The Arranged Wedding

Linda Louisa Dell

Copyright © 2014 Linda Louisa Dell

All rights reserved, including the right to reproduce this book, or portions thereof in any form. No part of this text may be reproduced, transmitted, downloaded, decompiled, reverse engineered, or stored, in any form or introduced into any information storage and retrieval system, in any form or by any means, whether electronic or mechanical without the express written permission of the author.

This is a work of fiction. Names and characters are the product of the author's imagination and any resemblance to actual persons, living or dead, is entirely coincidental.

Proof read by Sally-Ann McLaclan
www.checkpointproofreading.co.uk

ISBN: 978-1-326-12607-0

PublishNation, London
www.publishnation.co.uk

Other books by Linda Louisa Dell

Non fiction

Can't Sleep, Won't Sleep (Reasons and remedies for insomnia) Published by Capall Bann in, 2005

Dreamtime (A History, Mythology, Physiology and Guide to the Interpretation and A-Z of Dreams) Published by Capall Bann, 2008

Aphrodisiacs, Aphrodite's Secrets (Sexuality, Sexual Dysfunction and an A-Z, History and Anecdotal use of Aphrodisiacs) Published by Capall Bann, 2009

Mystic Moon (A history of the world's mythology surrounding the moon). To be published with Capall Bann publishing, www.capallbann.co.uk

Fiction

Yes and Pigs Might Fly (Rosie's Story). Published by emp3books, 2011

African Nights, Georgina's Story. Published by emp3books, 2011

The Story Tree, 30 short stories. Published by emp3books

Earthscape, A long way from home. Published by PublishNation 2012

Joke Book (Contains over a 120 Jokes). Published by PublishNation 2012

Aphrodisiacs an A-Z. Published by Skyhorse publishing New York, 2015

Available only on Amazon Kindle

Dream Dictionary (The complete A-Z of dreams and their meanings)

Unlock the Meanings to your Dreams

Dream Perspectives

Mothers and Children with Sleep Problems, Published by Bookopedia

For more information about Linda Louisa Dell and her other books, see her web page:

www.lindalouisadell.com

Excerpt from Leena Purri's diary (April 25th)

I can't believe it, how could they do this to me - and Rajput Gowda of all people? Why, all he thinks about is cars and computer games. Bloody hell, he gets on better with my brother than me and Seth is only thirteen. Well, that makes sense, Rajput acts about thirteen most of the time.

I don't want to get married. I want to go to university. And if I did want to marry, which I don't, not for years, it would not be to a stuck-up childish idiot like Rajput Gowda.

My parents must be crazy, well his family are rich, Dad is probably thinking about the business opportunities they can bring him. Are they living in the dark ages? Arranged marriages are so old. I won't do it. I won't, I won't, I won't. How could they agree to this; it's that meddlesome busybody Aunty Roopa, the bloody matchmaker; I knew she was up to something when the other day, she asked me what I was planning to do next ...'

Part One

Chapter One

"They didn't even think to ask me; they just came out with it. And they said it as if I should be pleased, over the moon or some such. No consideration for what I want to do with my life. I ask you!" Leena says, bursting with anger at her parents' dismissive behaviour towards her.

"That's parents for you *in' it*. They always think they know what's best for you. Take my mum she…" Pretti replies fiddling with her long dark hair as she speaks.

"And mum's no help," Leena interrupts, "she said, 'we only want what's best for you darling.' 'Going to university is what's best for me Mum,' I said, but she just doesn't listen."

"I know. My mum wants me to go to college to do pharmacy, but I want to learn how to be a beauty therapist. Dawn has had the most fabulous henna tattoo done, have you seen it? It's like a lizard, on her shoulder, *fab* it is, I think I might get one, except Mum would completely freak out. I thought she was going to have a heart attack when I got my belly ring…"

Leena interrupts Pretti again. "Pretti, you're not even listening to me. This is my life …"

"Yes I am. Your mum and dad want you to get married; so what, you will have to get married to someone one day… Who is it anyway?" Pretti asks, "Although my mum is in no hurry to marry me off to someone just now."

"You're lucky. Mine seem determined to get rid of me as soon as possible."

"My mum says get an education, a means of support, my dad has not always been that good at providing for us over the years. I think she wants to make sure I can fend for myself." Pretti shrugs. "I don't mind, I am in no hurry to get married, well not just yet."

"Perhaps we should swap parents. Yours seem to be more ..." Leena pauses, "amenable." She is maddened but realises that Pretti is not really listening. "It's busy today," she mutters looking around.

It is a bright, spring April day in the busy Kent market town of Tonbridge. The streets are full of bustle and noise. Four young girls are walking down the high street of the busy shopping centre. It is very crowded, full of shoppers come to town for the regular Saturday market.

The four girls are all about nineteen years old; two look Asian and two European. Walking slightly ahead is the first Asian girl. Pretti is very beautiful.

"I like Linda's top," Pretti says teetering on her high heeled shoes. She is wearing a dark green, skimpy tee-shirt with her mid-section revealing a gold belly button ring. She has a saucy swagger in her stride in her tight blue jeans. "Did she get it from Benji's stall?"

"I don't know, probably, he has some great things for sale this year. I saw a super shirt there the other day..." Leena answers.

"Linda always looks good, don't you think?" Pretti interrupts.

"Yes. I love that colour." Leena stops and looks around at the other two girls. "She looks very good in it."

Leena is just as attractive as Pretti but more demurely attired in black jeans, a pink cotton blouse and trainers, her long glossy hair is tied up in a ponytail.

"She sure does." Pretti replies. "I love that blue."

The two British girls are similarly attired in jeans and summer tops and they are laughing and giggling together as they move slightly apart from the two Asian girls. Linda, who is wearing a striking turquoise blouse with a threaded silvery design, is the typical English rose with blond hair and blue eyes; Fay is shorter with dark reddish-brown spiky hair and sparkling brown eyes. She is also wearing a short cotton blouse in a rusty-gold colour that really goes well with her glossy chestnut hair.

Leena and Pretti are well ahead of the two other girls and are now locked in conversation. Linda and Fay drop even further behind when they get distracted by a window display in a jewellery shop.

"What am I going to do?" Leena abruptly turns back to her friend. "Pretti, they just won't listen to me."

"I don't know, Leena. But ..."

"I can't marry him, I just can't."

"Who is it you are going to marry?" Pretti asks, returning to the subject of Leena's arranged wedding. "What's his name?"

"I'm not going to marry anyone," Leena replies. "I want to go to university; and I have already applied to Brighton."

"Who is it?" Pretti asks emphatically taking Leena's arm, a concerned look on her beautiful face.

"What?" Leena says.

"Who is it they want you to marry?" Pretti grasps Leena's arm, holding her still and looks pointedly into her eyes. "Who is it?"

"Oh, some boy they know from the social club, Rajput Gowda. I have only met him a couple of times. He is always off with the boys or playing computer games."

"Rajput Gowda?" Suddenly Pretti stops short and looks shocked; she turns her face away from Leena.

"Yes, do you know him? He's such a numbskull, never read a book, a complete cultural wasteland."

"Yes. No, I mean not well," she pauses. "I have seen him at the club of course."

Pretti is now looking very distracted and flustered and she gazes down at her feet while again twisting her long hair between her fingers.

"Are you okay, Pretti?" Leena asks. "You've gone very pale."

"Yes, but ..."

At that moment the two other girls re-join them and Leena's attention is distracted by the flashy new earrings that Linda has just purchased.

"Aren't they cool? I can wear them with that new outfit for Ted's party," Linda says twisting the earrings in her hand to show off the pretty silver and blue design.

"Oh Linda, I love them. What do you think, Leena?" Fay asks. "By the way, where's Dawn?

"I don't know, her mum said she was out when I knocked. They're gorgeous, is that turquoise?" Leena asks. "They will compliment your blue eyes and that lovely top."

"Yes, turquoise and silver, they're divine aren't they? I love them to bits. What do you think, Pretti?" Linda asks as she prances around her friend.

Linda holds up one of the earrings to her ear to demonstrate. They now come up to a stall in the road run by their friend, Benji. On the stall there are clothes, mostly tee-shirts and tracksuits but some Indian skirts and caftan-like garments and cotton shirts in lots of bright colours.

"Hi Benji, how are you?" Linda asks. "You got some nice new *garms*, in' it."

"Okay you know, but business is quiet today. Are you going to the party at Ted and Eve's?" he asks and looks around at a group of people walking past. "Lots of people but there're not spending any money."

"Yes, I am, should be a good night, I *reckon*. I just bought some earrings to wear; do you want to see them?" Linda asks Benji.

"I think they're great," Benji says, examining the earrings and then looking round at the other girls. "Dawn not with you?"

"No," Leena replies. "She's out with her dad or something."

"Right," says Benji with a shrug.

Benji is a good looking guy, about 5ft 11, slim and athletic in build. His deep-set brown eyes sparkle as he exchanges banter with the four girls. He is slightly older than them, around twenty seven and full of life but he is also known as a terrible gossip. If you want to find out what is happening in the town you ask Benji.

"Did you hear about the ruckus at the pub last night, some bloke got stabbed?" Benji asks. "He's okay, but will have a nasty scar; it was all about some girl or something, in' it?"

"Yes," Linda replies. "She's a right *skeet*, was in my class at school. I don't know the guy well but he is a bit wild by all accounts."

"Gabby her name is, in' it? Short for Gabriella I think." Fay shrugged. "A right little *poser*, I'm not surprised she's in trouble, terrible little flirt at school as I remember." Fay turned away to look at a rail of Indian cotton blouses.

During this exchange while the other girls are talking to Benji, Pretti stays very quiet and does not engage with the others. Leena turns to her friend to examine her face but is distracted by Linda who is now holding up a bright red shirt in front of her and pirouetting about the stall.

Fay laughs and nudges her friend. "Benji's got some good *garms, in' it*. I love it, Linda," she says. "You should be a model."

Fay and Leena start looking at the Indian cotton shirts on the rail.

"Look," Leena says. "I like this one."

"I have a joke," Benji says, "*ma mandem*."

"Yes, my friend, we've heard your corny jokes before," Linda says. "Okay let's have it."

"What is the definition of a mistress?" Benji asks looking hurt, but with a mischievous glint in his eye.

"Okay, what is the definition of a mistress?" Linda asks.

"It's something that comes between a master and his mattress."

"Oldie but a goody!" Linda groans and turns to Leena who laughs.

"That's a good one," Leena says and turns back to the rail of clothes. "I like this skirt as well. What do you think, Pretti? Hey, you okay?"

Leena notices that Pretti is looking upset and very agitated and she is fiddling with her mobile phone as if she wants to make a call, but does not want to do it in front of her friends. Eventually, while her friends are occupied looking at Benji's merchandise, she starts to move away.

"Super, look I have to go," she says offhandedly, hiding her face. Pretti then walks off and leaves the other girls standing watching her hunched back as she retreated.

"Hey Pretti," Linda shouts. "Where's she going?"

"I don't know, she's been acting funny," Leena says. "She's upset about something. Has been all morning."

"What's her problem, Leena?" Fay asks, turning to Leena.

"That girl has got something on her mind," Benji says. Benji also looks towards the fleeing Pretti and a knowing look crosses his face, but then he is distracted by a woman coming on to his stall and looking at the cotton shirts.

"I'm not sure, we were just talking and then she just went a bit odd. She has seemed a bit distracted all morning, not really listening to what I was saying," Leena says.

"You don't think she is still seeing that guy do you? You know, the teacher?" Fay asks. "She's very jumpy"

"Yes, like a box of frogs!" Benji quips.

No, I'm sure that's over," Leena says giving Benji a sidewise look, "but I think there may be someone else, she has been very secretive lately!"

"Her mum nearly had a heart attack over that teacher guy. But nothing really happened, it was just a crush, and he led her on, men!" Fay shrugs. "It is bound to be a man. With Pretti it's always a man, in' it. She's a bit of a *fronter* at times."

"Oh Fay, she's not that bad. Well, yes perhaps she is," Leena laughs. "But … he's gone now, that teacher, and they are not in contact as far as I know.

"Oh well, she's always so wrapped up in her own world. Let's go and get a coffee down at that new place, Finch House, before we go home. I want to tell you all about this great boy I met at college and my new outfit for the party," Linda says putting her earrings away. "Are you coming tonight, Leena? Bye Benji, see you at the party."

"If I can get away; you know what my parents are like," Leena says. "Did I tell you that they want me to get married in June? I just can't do it; I want to go to university…"

"Are you coming, Leena?" Fay asks not really listening, "for a coffee?"

"No, I'd better get going, I want to go and see Dawn and I might try and find Pretti, see what's eating her," Leena replies.

"Laters," Linda says. "See you Benji."

"Yes *laters*," Fay echoes. "See you at the party tonight."

The girls move off and wave goodbye to Benji who is watching a customer who is looking at the tee-shirts. He waves at their retreating backs and turns to help the lady who now also has a couple of cotton shirts in her hand.

"He's nice that Benji; I'm glad he's in our *crew*," Fay says, "funny that he doesn't fancy Indian girls."

"English girls are easier," Leena replies, with a smile.

"Hey," Fay says, "well I suppose it's true. We don't have the same restrictions as you, do we?"

"Not by a long way," Leena says, "not by a long, long way."

"It can't be easy juggling two cultures," Linda remarks.
"It certainly isn't. Well, I'll be off home now," Leena says.
"I think he is in love with Dawn," Fay said.
"Yes, he's always asking after her, *ain't* he?" Linda said.

Leena stops to look around trying to see where Pretti has gone and does not hear the comment about Dawn.

"I will phone Pretti tonight to see what's bothering her. If she'll talk that is."

"Okay, I'll catch up with you tomorrow," Fay replies.

"Bye Leena," Linda says, "try to come to the party."

The three girls part company. Leena heads back up towards the station and Linda and Fay continue off down the road talking. They do not notice that in a small alleyway between some shops Pretti is standing talking animatedly into her mobile phone, she looks extremely unhappy, in fact she is crying.

Chapter Two

The following morning Leena carrying a laundry basket, rushed into the garden pursued by her mother. Leena began to hang washing on to the line while her mother looked on in exasperation.

"Hey, there's still a stain on my *trackies*," Leena said as she held up her new grey track suit bottoms and nearly knocked over the basket of still wet washing.
"Be careful girl," Rani said. "You're not competing ... it's not a race."
Rani was plump and round faced, she was dressed in a traditional sari in a lovely pale blue colour, Leena was wearing a loose, dark blue tracksuit and her hair was tied was up in a ponytail.
"Really mum, I don't want to get married."
"Of course you do, Leena don't be silly. That's what all girls want a husband and babies. We only want what is best for you Leena. He's a nice boy from a good family," Rani scolded. "He seems perfectly presentable to me, and from a very good family. Aunty Roopa says that they are very wealthy ... he's handsome, you have to agree and polite. Don't you want children of your own?"
"No, I don't want a family until I am older, much older and after I've got a degree and a good job," Leena interrupted, then paused and turned to her mother, her face set in a stubborn scowl. "Oh yes, he's perfectly presentable! You mean, his family, they are rich, and they are a good business contact for dad."
She then turned back to the washing and started frantically hanging items on the line.
"How can you say that? Your father loves you and wants you to be happy?"
"I won't be happy with this boy. I don't love him, and I won't marry him," Leena said, her back stiff in indignation. As she talked Leena jerked the washing basket and it overturned spilling some of its contents onto the lawn.

"Take care girl or we'll have to wash those shirts again, your dad can't go to work covered in grass stains. - You don't know him Leena. You will grow to love Rajput like I did your father," Rani said looking on at Leena in exasperation.

"I will not grow to love him, because I will not marry him."

"What's so wrong with him?"

Leena stopped, picked up the fallen shirts and then she turned towards her mum.

"Where do I start? He's stupid and old fashioned; all he wants is an ornament on his arm..." she paused, "an unpaid secretary, cook and cleaner in his parents' house. I will be nothing more than cheap labour to the family business. Mum you must understand?"

"That's not true, he has a good job running his own business and Aunty Roopa says that he's modern minded and looking for an intelligent wife."

"Yes, he is looking for an intelligent wife so he does not have to work too hard and yes, he is broad minded. From what I hear he is screwing any pretty girl that will have him."

"Leena watch your mouth; the neighbours will hear you." Rani looked shocked and gazed around as if there was someone hiding in the bushes, but then she shot back with. "Sevi likes him."

"Sevi would like him; they are about the same mental age and they ... and they both like computer games and cars..." Leena threw down the part empty washing basket and stood hands on hips and shouted defiantly. "I don't want to get married Mum. Can't you understand that?"

"Leena have you gone mad?" Rani pointed at the washing and glared; it was her special 'listen to me, I'm your mother and I know best' glare.' "It's what we are here for, us women, to get married and have children. Look after our men."

"No it isn't, times are changing," Leena said. "We can have a life now, our own life, a career, and not be tied down to a family."

"I don't feel as if I haven't had a life, I've been happy and that's all I want for you my baby girl."

""Oh Mum ... It's pointless, how can I try to explain."

"Do you think my life has been pointless? Leena I have given up everything for you and Sevi. But I don't feel as if I have missed out on anything..."

"Mum, I did not mean …"
"Well your father has decided, so the marriage will go ahead."
"No Mum, it won't," Leena said. "I refuse…"
"We have made up our minds Leena. Please be a good girl"
"Mum," Leena groaned, then she quickly twisted away and picked up the clothes from the basket and sorted them to hang up on the line, keeping her face turned away from her mother, so that she could not see the tears of frustration that were teeming down her face. "No," Leena answered, her voice almost inaudible, "I won't marry him; you can't make me."

Having hung all the clothes erratically on the line Leena threw down the peg bag and stormed off back into the house. Rani followed her with the empty clothes basket and peg bag looking exasperated and confused. She was looking around to see if Mrs Price was around. Rani knew that her neighbour could not resist a good bit of gossip.

"What are we going to do with this girl?" she asked herself. "Oh Leena, she is so obstinate, just like her father."

Chapter Three

"Where did you go yesterday?" Leena asked Pretti as she stood at the window; she looked agitated. "Did you go to Ted's party?"

It was the day following the big party. Pretti and Leena were in Leena's bedroom; there were posters of pop stars on the wall and all the usual paraphernalia of a teenager was scattered around in the pretty room with its primrose yellow walls and gold and orange patterned curtains and bedspread to match. Pretti sat on the bed and she was nervously pushing back her long hair with one hand while the other caressed a pretty golden coloured cushion.

"No, I didn't." Pretti paused. "This is beautiful," she said indicating the cushion which had sparkly threads in blue, silver and gold and red stones and shiny mirrors embroidered into its cover.
"Yes," Leena replied distractedly. "My mum brought it back from India, last time she visited Aunty Lakshmi. Where did you rush off to?"
"I," Pretti mumbled and she picked up the lovely cushion and held it in her lap, "I needed to go somewhere."
"Go where?"
"I went for a walk round the castle."
"The castle! Whatever for? Leena asked. "I wanted to talk to you about this bloody arranged wedding and you just ran off."
"Sorry," Pretti said quietly not lifting her eyes from the cushion.

Leena sprang away from the window and paced backwards and forwards. She marched over to her dressing table and started picking up things and putting them down again. Suddenly Leena turned to Pretti.

"I don't know what to do ..." Leena said. I ..."
"Nor do I," Pretti interrupted. "I have to tell you something, Leena."

"Yes, we need to talk, I know you were upset yesterday, and that something is bothering you. But I'm in such a state about this wedding business. I can't think straight." Leena paused. "I am sorry if I'm being insensitive Pretti, what's wrong?"

"I had to see someone, talk to someone," she mumbled. "Anyway... why are you in such a state?" Pretti asked.

"I had a terrible row with my mum this morning," Leena said resuming her pacing.

"About this – this arranged wedding?" Pretti replied. "Have your parents made any arrangement? I mean have you met his parents or what?"

"No." Leena stopped walking and went over to sit on the bed next to Pretti.

Pretti seemed very subdued; she was hiding her face as she again ran her fingers over the cushion.

"How can they do this to me? I want to go to university and make something of my life. It's not fair. Pretti, I want more from life than babies and ... I don't want to marry this boy."

"It's not so bad," Pretti said quietly. "He's very good looking and comes from a rich family. You needn't go to work." She paused and looked up at Leena for the first time. "But if you don't want to," her voice was very low and unresponsive, "but... if you don't want to marry him you will have to make a stand, it won't be easy, but I ..."

Leena was not really listening and continued her ranting.

"But, I want to work. I want a career. I don't want to sit around all day reading magazines, cooking and waiting for my husband to come home. Aunty Roopa says he is broadminded. But I have heard stories that he just uses any girl who will let him put his hand up her skirt."

"Oh, that's not fair," Pretti said looking very uncomfortable. "He's not that bad."

"Why are you defending him?"

"Oh, no reason, but if you are really against this marriage maybe you should put your foot down and refuse to get married."

"It's no use; they have made up their mind. They don't care about my feelings or about what I want."

Leena stood up again and marched about the room once more; she picked up a silk scarf from a chair and started to run it through her fingers.

"I can't believe it, how could they do this to me? Rajput Gowda of all people? Why, all he thinks about is cars and computer games. Bloody hell, he gets on better with my brother than me. And Sevi is only thirteen. Well that makes sense: Rajput acts about thirteen most of the time. I don't want to get married. I want to go to university. And if I did want to marry, which I don't, not for years, it would not be to a stuck up childish idiot like Rajput Gowda. My parents must be crazy, well his family are rich and dad is probably thinking about the business opportunities. Are they living in the Dark Ages? Arranged marriages are so old, I won't do it. I won't, I won't. How could they agree to this? It's that bloody Aunty Roopa, that bloody match-maker ... I knew she was up to something when the other day, she asked me what I was..."

"Your parents always think they know what's best for you," Pretti said quietly.

"If I hear one more person say that, I will scream. What is best for me is to go to university and to make something of my life." Leena stood very still and looked down at Pretti, and as she talked she was tying the scarf into knots. "I don't want to get married...."

"Yes, well..." Pretti started to say.

"Why can't they understand that I want more from my life than..."

"Let's go shopping. That will cheer you up," Pretti said interrupting and trying to look a bit more animated. "I need to buy a new lipstick and we could ask Dawn, I know she wants to see the new shirts that Benji has just ..."

"Buying more make-up is not the answer to everything Pretti," Leena said bitterly.

"Okay. Okay. But don't take it out on me. I haven't done anything wrong..." But as Pretti said this she looked down quickly, her face reddened and tears came to her eyes.

When Pretti turned her face away from Leena she looked decidedly guilty and uncomfortable, as she tried to hide the tears from Leena. Leena threw down the now mangled silk scarf and went over to Pretti and put her hand on her shoulder.

"Oh, I'm sorry Pretti, it's not your fault," Leena said. "I'm in such a bad temper. Let's go to the cinema that will take my mind off all this mess. What was it you wanted to talk about? You said you had something to tell me."

"Oh, it's not important," Pretti stammered. "It can wait."

"You're sure?"

"Yes, let's go out. What do you want to go and see?" Pretti sat up and scooped her hair back from her face for the first time, and pushed the pretty cushion off her lap. She looked slightly happier as she looked up at Leena.

"The new Hugh Grant film is supposed to be very good," Pretti said.

"Fine, I think that's on at the new Complex. Let's go now so we can stop to see Benji first. He has some new skirts in from India."

"You like Benji, don't you?" Pretti asked.

"Yes, I like Benji, but I don't fancy him. Anyway my parents would not find him suitable, being in trade. They are such snobs. New stock; I saw some very pretty shirts yesterday. Okay, let's go and have a look but I can't afford to buy anything," Leena said, grabbing up her handbag. "Let's go."

"Okay," Pretti said and turned to get her own bag. As they descended the stairs they were intercepted by Leena's mum.

"Hello Pretti. How's the family?" Rani asked.

"Fine thank you, Mrs Purri. And you?" Pretti asked.

"Good," she said, darting a glance at Leena and handing her a couple of envelopes. "Post these for me Leena. Have a good time you two and don't be too late in. Bye now. See you later. Leena, don't forget that we are having company next week. I want you to put on that nice sari we gave you last year for Diwali." Mrs Purri turned to Pretti, "Leena's going to meet her betrothed on Saturday."

"Oh Mum," Leena groaned. "I don't want to wear a sari."

"Leena ..." Mrs Purri started to say but they were gone. Mrs Purri gazed at the closing door for a moment then she turned away and shrugged her shoulders. "She will come round," Mrs Purri said with a sigh. "I know she will."

Chapter Four

"I'll just pop in next door and see if Dawn's coming out," Pretti said heading towards Dawn's front door.

"Okay, I'll wait here," Leena said leaning against the gate with a sigh of relief.

When Pretti knocked at the Prices' door it was opened by Dawn's older brother, Alistair.

"Hello Pretti," he said. "What can I do for you?"

Alistair was tall, dark and good looking, with brown eyes that were narrow, deep set and shadowy and always seemed to be hiding something. His hair was beautiful, shoulder length and a glossy, vibrant chestnut-red; the same as his sister, Dawn's. He was wearing blue jeans and a black jacket over a pale blue shirt. He looked good and he knew it. He always had a cocky look about him and walked with that hips forward sort of swagger that many over confident young men seemed to have.

"Is Dawn in?" Pretti asked. Alistair always made her feel slightly uncomfortable; he was always pleasant, even too nice, in a smarmy way that made her feel as if she had trodden in something nasty.

"Want to see her?" he asked, a strange leery grin on his face. "I'm just leaving." Then he saw Leena waiting by the gate. "I'll go talk to Leena, take your time, girly."

"Right," Pretti said, and entered the house calling for Dawn.

Alistair bounded down the path towards Leena and immediately took her arm. He stood far too close and his presence felt intimidating. He smelled of some exotic aftershave, which was far too strong.

"So what's this I hear about you getting married?" he asked.

"Not if I can help it," Leena said backing away.

"That's not what I heard."

"Well, Mum and Dad want me to, but …"

"So, are you, like, promised to someone then?"

"No," Leena said; she felt alarmed. Alistair was odd and he scared her. She knew that he had left home under strange circumstances and she never felt very comfortable in his company. "I don't intend to get married, not just yet. I want to go to university. But Mum and Dad have arranged ..."

"So are you getting married?"

"No," Leena said. "Dad wants me to but..."

"What does that mean?"

"It's not settled," she replied.

"So you can choose?" he said.

Leena shook her head.

"Could you marry a white guy?" he asked. "Or ..."

"No," Leena said, "white, black and definitely not Muslim."

"Could you date one?"

"What?"

"Could you date a white guy?"

"Well..."

"Want to come out with me? We could go for meal or something."

"I don't know what you're on about, are you asking me out?" Leena was shaking her head.

"Well, yes, I guess I am, how about it?"

Alistair moved closer to her again and Leena stepped back.

"I don't have time to go with boys who just want one thing. I don't sleep around; I'm going to university to make something of my life."

Alistair burst out laughing, "That's a good one," he said. "You're a poppet."

At that moment Pretti exited the Prices' front door and gave Leena and Alistair a strange look.

"She's not coming, has to do something with her father, said to say hi," Pretti said.

"Well. I'll be off, remember what I said Leena, anytime," Alistair said. "Nice to see you Pretti, Leena. *Laters*," he yelled as he bounded over to his nifty little sports car and raced away.

"What was that all about?" Pretti asked.

"He asked me out," Leena said. "He really gives me the creeps.

"No!" Pretti exclaimed, "He has a terrible reputation. They say he's into drugs and all sorts of stuff. I'd keep away from him if I were you."

"I wouldn't touch him with a barge pole," Leena said with a shudder. "He's weird and not in a good way."

"Too right," Pretti said and then she took Leena's arm and they moved off down the street. "He's a bit freaky!"

Chapter Five

The Purri family lived on a small suburban street near Tonbridge station; the houses had small narrow back gardens and Mrs Purri was right to be concerned about her neighbour overhearing her arguing with her Leena the previous day. Mrs Price loved nothing better than to hear some good, juicy gossip.

"You'll never believe what I just heard," Mrs Price said calling out to her husband as she entered her kitchen.
"What love?" her mousy husband asked as he helped himself to another cup of tea from the pot and then ran his hand through his hair. His eyes were weary and resigned, he leaned back in his chair and tried to look interested, but although his face reflected concern his mind was elsewhere. He was thinking about his life and what had become of the promising young man he had been, as he looked up at his wife in her unbecoming wraparound pinafore.
Mrs Price was a large woman, domineering and loud. She went straight to the sink and began to wash some potatoes for their lunch. She had short, permed, dark brown hair with the start of grey at the temples and a stern steely look in her hazel eyes.

"Rani and Leena were in the garden hanging out some washing. Well, Leena was hanging the washing. Very untidily too, I might add, and they were discussing a wedding. I was just coming in from the gazebo with these potatoes but when I heard them talking. I ... well, I just waited to see what ... well, if there is going to be a wedding I need to know about it, don't I?" Joan Price paused as if thinking about what she had heard and her husband waited patiently, he knew she would get around to telling him in her own time and did not want to rile her by asking her to get to the point. He had learned years ago to just listen and not speak back if he wanted a quiet life.
"Yes dear," he said and waited for her to continue.
"Well, Mrs Purri. Her name's Rani you know! She was saying that they had decided that Leena was going to get married. And

Leena's not very happy about it; she said that she was not going to get married to some playboy," Mrs Price paused. "Can you imagine, George? Then Leena threw down the washing basket and stalked off into the house. Like a right little madam. And then Rani followed her into the house muttering to herself - that woman is really putting on weight."

"Poor girl," George said. "I expect it's difficult for ..."

"Well, it's their culture, isn't it? Can't say I agree, but if that's the way they do things, it's not up to us to *intersect*, even if we don't agree with it. Even Alistair has heard something. He said so on the phone yesterday. He's coming over later..."

"Interfere," George said ignoring the reference to their eldest son.

"What?" Joan snapped as she put the potatoes into the oven to roast.

"It's interfere, not intersect," George said quietly. "We can't do anything..."

"Well, I am sure you are right, I mean what would I know? I never went to college, did I? Fat lot of good it did you," she said snidely. "With no job..."

"I did not mean..." George started to say belatedly realizing that he had put his foot in it again. Joan hated to be contradicted in any way and since he had lost his job the year before she had become very bitter and sarcastic. He had an education, a degree in science but it did not help him find a job. Or if he found one it only lasted a short time. With cuts to education budgets it's last in first out and modest Mr Price always seems to be the target for the first redundancies. Jean, who had no higher education, made ends meet by working as a dinner lady down at the comprehensive school.

"I mean, I left school at fifteen, but it falls to me to feed the family, doesn't it?" she continued splashing away at the unfortunate vegetables in the sink. "I hope our kids do better. Dawn gets too distracted by her so-called friends. At least Alistair is making something of himself; did you see his lovely new car?"

"Dawn is doing well at school, isn't she?" George said. "You like Leena and her friends Pretti, Linda and Fay. They seem like nice girls."

"They're all right, I guess; if you like bubble-headed bimbos with only two things on their minds; boys and clothes. They wear strappy little tops and tight jeans, and have dyed hair and streaky highlights. Leena is okay but that Pretti thinks she's some Bollywood starlet."

"But our Dawn ..."

"Our Dawn needs to get her head down, and not be distracted by those trollops."

"Yes," George said, "but that's a bit harsh."

Mrs Price glared at her husband but George just averted his eyes and kept quiet. He was a tall slim man with receding hair that was a dark, rusty red in colour, which he had passed on to his children.

"Make yourself useful and get Jim moving, if he don't get a shift on he will be late for his football practice."

"Yes dear," he said. George was pleased to have an excuse to get away from his hectoring wife so he scuttled out into the hall way. "Jim, move yourself or you will be late for football training," he yelled up the stairs. "Dawn darling."

George loved his daughter very much. She was everything that his wife was not. She had inherited his red hair and sparkling blue eyes, she was intelligent and articulate and she was going to go to college in September and he was so proud. The two youngsters bounded down the stairs, twelve year old Jim pushing his older sister out of the way as he passed her knocking a book out of her hand.

"Careful, Jim," she said bending to scoop it up.

"Get out of the way then, sis, I'm hungry."

"You're always hungry," she said laughing.

"Got to keep up me energy, don't I?" Jim was a greedy boy but very athletic so he remained fairly slim.

"I'd say you have enough energy for two boys," Dawn said.

"He seems to eat for two," George quipped, getting out of the way of his boisterous son. "Your mum's heard that Leena is getting married," George said as he stood at the bottom of the stairs facing his daughter.

"No," Dawn said, "she told me she was going to university in September.

"Married, dad? What on earth does she want to get married for?" Jim exclaimed.

"Well, the thing is, I don't think she does want to get married. Mum overheard Leena arguing with her mum about it in the garden."

"I'll ask Sevi about it on the way to football," Jim said. "He'll know."

"Poor Leena," Dawn said pausing to give her father a kiss on the cheek. "You would never force me to get married would you, Pops?" she asked.

"No darling, I never want you to leave home."

"George," Joan's voice yelled from the kitchen," what are you doing out there? I want some shopping and as you have nothing better to do you can go …"

Dawn smiled timidly at her father.

"Something will turn up, Dad. Your luck will change, I just know it."

"Yes, my darling girl, it will," George said reluctantly following his lovely slim daughter into the kitchen. "My darling girl," he said softly to himself, "don't ever leave."

George adored his daughter, was fond of his younger son, and preferred not to think about Alistair, but he only tolerated his wife, she was once a lovely, tall, long limbed girl. The years had soured her; her large frame was now intimidating and repulsive to him. And she grew stronger as he grew weaker. 'If only I still had my job. I loved that job, I had respect then,' he thought.

"Stop daydreaming and set the table," his wife yelled.

"Yes dear," he said meekly winking at his daughter.

"Humph," she grunted.

Chapter Six

The following Saturday afternoon came far too quickly for Leena and there was an uncomfortable miasma in the air in the living room of the Purri family home. Mr Purri sat on the sofa with a determined look on his face and Rani ran backwards and forwards, first with duster in hand, then bringing in food and generally panicking. Leena sat resolute and sulky in her best silk sari feeling trapped and desperate. She looked resentfully around at her mother and refused to talk to her father.

"Stop worrying, Rani, it'll be okay," Mr Purri said as his wife buzzed around the room, plates of savouries in her hands. Leena and her father both looked grim. "What is that boy doing?" The sound of a computer game came from the next room.
"Sevi, stop that. Come in here before they arrive. Sevi do you hear me?" Rani yelled, but then she turned to Lion. "What's the matter with that boy?" she said more quietly addressing her husband.
"Sevi," Mr Purri yelled. "Listen to your mother,"
"All right, all right, I hear you," Sevi said. "I'll be there in a minute."
"Come in here now Sevi," she shouted. "I won't ask you again."

Sevi put his head around the door, an ill-humoured expression on his face as he looked over at his sister and father. Sevi's father sat woodenly next to Leena on the bumpy old sofa and not in his usual comfy chair. Lion had an anxious expression on his face.
It was a comfortable modern living room with two sofas, two arm chairs and a large wooden coffee table; there were lots of pictures on the magnolia coloured walls.

"Do I have to? He's not going to marry me is he? I want to finish this game. I'm on level three already," he said through the door as he disappeared once again.

"Get in here now!" Lion yelled. "Just do as your mother says for once." Lion turned to Rani who was coming in the door with yet another plate of sandwiches. "That boy spends too much time in front of that computer."

"Okay, okay, don't get your knickers in a twist. I'm sure lover boy will not even see me when he claps his eyes on Princess Leena," Sevi yelled back. "I'm just turning off the computer."

Lion Purri was a large man, over six feet tall and big boned, as his wife would say. He had a flowing mop of wavy dark hair that he wore swept back from his brow; his eyes were usually kind and sensitive but this particular afternoon his jaw was set in a firm angle. He could be stubborn but he loved his family very much and was convinced that he would always do the best for them; even if they did not always agree with him.

Sevi came into the room and threw himself into the corner of the second sofa, a surly look on his face. Normally a cheerful, good natured and pleasant looking boy, Sevi had inherited his father's mane of unruly hair and his mother's dark expressive eyes. This day he too looked resentful and edgy. His eyes slid to Leena, but her gaze was closed and introspective. He shrugged and then he looked down at his feet, trying to conceal, in front of his parents, the empathy he felt for his sister.

He went to grab one of the pastries that his mum had bought specially but Rani smacked his hand away.

"Those are for our guests," she said, "and don't talk to your father like that, and don't tease Leena, she's nervous enough already. It's about time you started to act your age, you are twelve… you're not a child anymore."

"Sorry princess, I mean sis," Sevi said, grinning at Leena.

She had reluctantly worn her best sari, which was gold and lilac with silver and gold threads running through it. She looked very beautiful. Rani had insisted that she wear her shiny, long hair loose about her shoulders, not tied up in a ponytail the way she usually preferred. Brother and sister were still exchanging a nervous smile when the doorbell chimed and Sevi jumped up to get it.

"No Sevi, I will go. You just behave yourself," Rani said, pushing him back into his seat on the sofa and going towards the front door to usher in their visitors.

Leena groaned and looked at Sevi who pulled a face. Then Leena smiled and put her tongue out at Sevi just as Mr and Mrs Gowda entered with Rajput, Aunty Roopa, followed by a worried looking Rani. Mr Purri stood, lifting his ample frame from the sofa as they entered and marshalled everybody to a seat.

"Welcome to our home. This is my wife Rani, our son Sevi and our daughter Leena," Lion said.

"May I present Mr and Mrs Gowda and their son Rajput?" Aunty Roopa said; she was also dressed traditionally in a sari. Roopa was a cheerful, chubby woman with dark expressive eyes, large framed spectacles and red lipstick which matched the dark stain on her forehead.

Rajput nodded at Mr and Mrs Purri. He was looking around the room, his glance briefly resting on Leena as if assessing her. A handsome boy, with an arrogant look, glossy, straight hair and striking, almond shaped eyes; he was dressed in immaculately pressed, beige jeans and a caramel coloured silk shirt, that Leena thought must have cost a fortune. He did not smile at her; in fact, she sensed that he looked just as uncomfortable to be there as she felt having him there.

The Gowda family were dressed up in their finery, expensive but casual clothes, Mrs Gowda in a flowery western dress with lots of gold jewellery, Mr Gowda in a smart brown suit but with no tie.

Sevi thought that they looked ostentatious and he discreetly winked again at Leena while they were all getting comfortable.

"I'm pleased to meet you Mr and Mrs Purri, Sevi, Leena," Rajput said shaking hands with Mr Purri and then sitting down next to Sevi on the sofa. "You alright, Sevi?"

"Yes fine," Sevi replied, "and you?" But then he noticed the dirty look his father threw at him and went quiet.

"Would you like something to drink? There are savouries and sandwiches, please help yourself. I'm making tea," Rani said, offering the plate of delicate egg and cress sandwiches to Mrs Gowda.

"Tea would be nice, thank you very much," she said taking a sandwich gingerly and looking inside to see what the filling was before putting it down on to the small china plate that Rani had given her. "Do you have Earl Grey?"

"Tea for me too, Rani," Roopa said. "These look lovely," she indicated the tray of sandwiches.

"Thank you, Roopa. Mr Gowda, Rajput?" Rani asked. "Is tea okay? Do you want Earl Grey?"

"Yep… well I'd prefer a coke if you have one," Rajput said.

"Tea is fine for me," Mr Gowda said. "Rajput will have what he is given."

"Tea all round then," Rani said nervously.

Rajput and Mr Gowda both nodded to indicate that they would also have a cup of tea. Once they were all settled and seated comfortably Lion turned to Rajput.

"How are you getting on in the world? Making a name for yourself?"

"Okay, I suppose," Rajput replied. "I would like to travel; maybe I'll organize a supply chain from India. Bring in some new items."

"We are doing nicely with what we import now. No need to be hasty," Mr Gowda said. Rajput made a face at his father. "Rajput, please behave yourself …"

"But father …" Rajput started to say, "I can…"

"This is not the time or the place Rajput. Talk to Leena, she is going to be your wife. Get to know her."

Rajput turned to Leena, but said nothing. He just looked away and raised his eyebrows, he looked bored and sullen.

"Kids today, they are so impatient. Think they can run before they can walk. Don't you agree, Mr Purri?" Mr Gowda said.

"Oh yes, they do have some funny ideas these days, to be sure," Mr Purri replied. "My old mum would have a fit if she could remember anything for more than a few minutes."

"How is she?" Roopa asked. "Dementia, I think you said."

"Yes, she can't remember anything unless it happened forty years ago. Sometimes she thinks she's still in India," Mr Purri shrugged. "She has to go to the hospital every couple of months. At Christmas she had a stroke and her memory is now very bad," he said addressing Mr Gowda.

"Two weeks ago she had to go for a memory check. The doctor asked her if she knew the name of the Prime Minister. 'No,' mother said. "Well, don't worry, the doctor replied, I will tell you a story. The Prime Minister was visiting a retirement home. He walked around talking to the old people and then he saw this little old lady sitting on her own by the window. He went over to her and said. Hello, my dear, do you know my name?"

She looked up at him.

"No," she replied, "why don't you go and ask at reception."

Mrs and Mrs Gowda laughed politely but Roopa looked up with a puzzled expression on her face.

"Is she in a home?" she asked, "your mum?"

"No, she lives with my younger sister Kalpane and her family in St Albans," Mr Purri said. "We see her nearly every week or so but unfortunately she doesn't remember us most of the time."

"How sad," Roopa said.

At that moment Rani returned to the room with a tray of cups and handed them out to her guests. She could tell that the atmosphere was strained and looked pointedly at her husband. Leena and Rajput seemed to be looking anywhere in the room except at each other.

"Give Rajput a cup of tea, Leena," she said, but Leena seemed in her own world and just ignored her.

"Leena," Mr Purri said sternly, "give the boy a cup of tea."

Leena slowly reached for the tray of teas, took a cup and saucer and handed it to Rajput, who nodded silently. Mr Gowda looked at him sharply and Rajput turned to Leena.

"Thank you, Leena," he muttered.

"You're welcome," she replied.

Lion turned towards Rajput again once they were all served but Rani was nervously staying very still, watching her guests, warily, standing in front of the kitchen door. She was feeling slightly uncomfortable; she had insisted that Leena wore a sari and she was herself decked out in her finest silk sari, yet Mrs Gowda had come in a summer dress, a very fine and probably very expensive summer dress, but a dress nonetheless ... Rani felt old-fashioned and awkward, she was so nervous and Leena and Rajput hardly looked at each other. Rani watched them all uneasily as she went to sit next to her son.

"What's your line, Rajput?" Lion asked politely.

"What?" Rajput said distractedly as he juggled his cup of tea and china plate with its little pile of sandwiches; he was looking over at Mr Purri in an indifferent way.

"What's your trade?" Lion said. "What line of work are you in?"

"Oh," he muttered, "I work in import and export. I have my own business, Mr Purri ... part of the family firm."

"What do you import and export?" Rani asked trying to elicit some animation in the boy. "Do you sell ...?"

"Oh, this and that, you know, Mrs Purri, this and that," Rajput said, as he looked briefly over at Rani. He looked bored; he was barely being civil until his father gave him a second stern look.

"My son is doing very well in business. He has just bought a new car; a new Jaguar," Mrs Gowda said as she cast a proud glance at her son and then turning her eyes to Leena and Mrs Purri.

"You've got a new Jaguar! Oh, how wonderful. What colour? Can I see it? Please," Sevi asked jumping up from the sofa. "I love cars, I want ..."

"Silver, yes, come see, did I hear that you have the latest Fire Warrior game?" Rajput asked for the first time looking interested.

"Yes, do you want to have a go?" Sevi asked. "We could..."

"Now Sevi, I'm sure Rajput doesn't want to play computer games. He's here to meet Leena, not you," Rani said. "Don't be a pest ..."

"Oh Mum," Sevi started to say, but was silenced by a severe look from his father. Sevi and Rajput both sat there looking bored and uncomfortable. Leena watched with a disdainful expression on her face. She appeared to be near tears but blinked, held them back and turned towards the tray, helping herself to a cup of tea.

"How are you doing at school, Sevi?" Rajput asked.

"Okay," Sevi answered. "I like IT and media studies."

"What do you want to do?" he asked. "It's very difficult to get into the world of media, unless you know someone that is, *in' it*?"

"Yes. I'm not sure; maybe I'll test computer games or do some computer programming. But I'd like to do something creative. Invent

29

my own games or something." Sevi indicated Rajput's shirt and said, "Nice *garms, in' it*."

"Thanks, I got this shirt up in London, cost a bob or two. Not like the *butters tat*, these oldies sporting," he laughs. "Yes, Sevi, you *gotta* get a first degree right?" Rajput said. "Me *piddy* Kamel, he got a degree but he still looking for work, *in' it*," Rajput shrugged before continuing. "But he is bit of a *cookie*, at times."

"Me go to university? Suppose so," Sevi replied. "The teachers, they ain't no help neither, *in' it*. Leena, she's the bright one in the family."

"Do what interests you man, that my advice." Rajput said, ignoring the reference to Leena, "and then find something to fit it."

"Computers are taking over the world," Lion said, shaking his head and smiling at Mr Gowda. "I hate this street language they use. Why can't they speak the Queen's English like what we were taught?"

"Yes, one can't do anything these days if you don't know how to work a computer," Mr Gowda replied, glancing over at Leena and then at Rajput and Sevi disapprovingly.

Mrs Purri was looking at her son and then at Rajput, and her face was very confused.

"I agree. I can hardly understand what the kids are saying half the time," Mrs Purri replied. "Sevi. What's a *piddy*?"

"Mum, a *piddy* is a friend," Sevi mumbled, "*in' it*."

"What a silly word," she replied. "Why can't you just say 'friend'?"

"Whatever," Sevi shrugged.

"Even in the shops all the tills are computerized and they are always breaking down and then where are we?" Mrs Gowda said looking over at Mrs Purri.

"If terrorists really wanted to cripple this world all they would need to do would be to cut off the electricity," Mr Gowda said. "Everything would grind to a halt. Do you remember Neela when there were those power cuts in New York? All the flights were cancelled for hours. We were stuck in Mumbai airport for ten hours. It was horrific."

"Yes, Jemale," Mrs Gowda replied, "I do remember; it was awful."

"I know, it's all a bit beyond me, I must say," Rani said. "I have tried, but I can't get on with the things. I have managed to conquer emails and it is nice to be in contact with my sister in India, but things are changing so fast. And I just don't trust internet banking, I like to deal with real people and see a proper statement ..."

Sevi raised his eyebrows at his mum, disdainful at her lack of knowledge and understanding of computers. He then turned towards Rajput. "What computer do you have, does it have touch screen, cloud technology and Wi-Fi ..." Sevi asked.

"Well *yeah*!" Rajput replied.

"Okay you two, I can see you want to exchange computer jargon and stuff... just come back soon... We have things to discuss," Lion said.

Sevi and Rajput got up quickly and then disappeared into the front garden to look at Rajput's new car and to talk about cars and computer games.

"Boys and their toys," Mrs Gowda said and laughed.

"Yes, the bigger the boys, the bigger their toys! How old is Sevi anyway? I will be arranging his wedding soon," Roopa said.

Mrs Gowda, Mr Gowda, Roopa and Lion all laughed but Rani and Leena looked on silently, not smiling. In fact, Leena again looked close to tears.

"What car do you have, Mr Purri?" Mrs Gowda asked. "We are thinking of buying the new Fiat."

"Please call me Lion. I have an old Rover. Can't beat it, uses up petrol, but it's so reliable. I have never had a day's problem with it," Lion said. "Not ever."

Rani turned to Leena as the others continued with their own conversations.

"Come and help me with the food and a fresh pot of tea, Leena, will you?" Rani said quietly to her daughter. Leena got up and they left the room and went into the kitchen.

"Now my accountant tells me that I can..." Mr Gowda was saying.

Mrs Gowda watched the two women as they left the room and then looked pointedly at Roopa raising her eyebrows. Then she smoothed down her expensive silk dress and looked back smugly at her husband as he held court in front of Mr Purri.

Chapter Seven

In the kitchen Rani and Leena could still hear muffled voices from the sitting room and the sounds of the computer game starting up again in the front room. Rani made a fresh pot of tea and uncovered even more sandwiches that had been standing on the counter under a tea towel.

"What's the matter with you? You have hardly said a word?" Rani said. "Leena!"

"I'd nothing to say, he's not interested in me anyway," Leena replied looking sulky. She went over to the back door and started fiddling with her sari.

"Of course he is. He's just nervous that's all," Rani said.

"He needs a wife and I'll do mum; that's all there is to it."

"Oh Leena, how can you say that?" Rani turned to her daughter and was shocked at how pale and dejected she seemed.

"Look mum, can't you see he is more interested in playing computer games with Sevi than talking to me. I don't understand how you can ..." Leena said and waved her arm towards the front room nearly knocking over the milk jug with the tail of her sari. "Why did I have to wear this thing? Mrs Gowda is in a summer dress for heaven's sake," Leena said pulling at the material. "It's so bloody clumsy."

"But you look beautiful, Leena. Talk to him," Rani said, exasperation showing in her voice. "Try to get him to open up to you."

"I'll try mum, I'll try. But he's only interested in himself."

"Oh Leena..." Rani started to say. But she lapsed back into silence while she finished making the tea. Leena looked sullen and just stood gazing vacantly out of the window, her face pale and frozen, her eyes shining, wet with unshed tears.

"Will you take the sandwiches?" Rani said, passing Leena a tray.

"Yes mum. But I don't think they'll eat them. They have hardly touched the first lot."

"It's customary, isn't it? At least the pastries went well."

As they left the room Rani's face looked sad and she shook her head but she followed Leena back into the sitting room bearing the tea things. As they entered the room Rani put a big smile on her face. But she could tell that it wasn't going well.

Chapter Eight

Mr and Mrs Gowda and Lion were having an intense conversation about business.

"Well, I must say, the economy will have to improve or many small businesses will suffer," Lion said. "I know several people who are having a tough time of it at the moment."

"Yes, that's true; the government will have to do something. Tax breaks perhaps. Small business is the backbone of this country after all," Mr Gowda said.

As Leena and Rani entered the room and sat down, Roopa turned and spoke to them in a hushed voice as the men's conversation continued on behind them.

"Well, Leena what do you think of our Rajput? He's handsome, don't you think?" Roopa said smiling at the girl. "Such a catch for you …"

"Yes, I suppose so, Aunty Roopa, but he…" she started to say.

"And he has his own business too; he's a good match for your Leena, don't you think, Rani?" Roopa interrupted.

"He seems like a pleasant boy," Rani said, "but rather quiet, he has hardly spoken to Leena."

At this moment Rajput and Sevi re-entered the room still talking about the merits of a new computer game.

"You can't beat Castle Wolfenstein," Sevi said. "It's *mega*."

"Yes, that's true but Space Invader IV is a good game and the Desert Storm games are awesome," Rajput answered.

"Come now, Rajput, you have hardly spoken to Leena?" Mrs Gowda suddenly said turning away from the two men who were still talking business.

Rajput went and sat next to Leena and she offered him a sandwich from a nearby tray.

"No thank you, Leena. So tell me all about yourself?" he asked, trying to look interested.

"What do you want to know?" she replied.

"Are you working? What do you do?" he asked.

"I have a job in an insurance office but I'm going to university in September to take environmental economics," Leena said looking enthusiastic for the first time. "I have a provisional place."

"Oh, I didn't know about that, we will see ..." Rajput said, glancing around at his parents. Mr Gowda, who had heard this last remark, shrugged his shoulders.

"What does a woman need a university degree for?" he laughed, "If she's only going to cook and have babies."

Leena pulled a face and turned to her brother, who giggled.

"You don't have to work. We have enough money for you to stay home with the children ... You can help us with the paperwork. And then ..." Mrs Gowda started to say.

"I want to have an education," Leena said in a stilted voice, "and I want to earn my own money and not be dependent on anybody." Leena sat indignant and cross but she lowered her eyes when her father frowned at her.

"Leena," he said sternly, "be polite ..."

"Leena is a modern young lady and she is intelligent," Roopa said quickly smiling at Mrs Gowda condescendingly. "She can contribute to..."

"Leena, we're a traditional family and the women stay home and help the household," Mrs Gowda said her face darkening in anger. "We don't mind you getting an education. But going away to university? What about the local college?"

"I'm sure Leena will make a good wife, Mrs Gowda," Rani started to say but she looked around at her daughter who was barely keeping the tongue in her mouth she was so furious.

"Yes, Leena dear, why work if you don't have to, you can..." Roopa started to say.

"I want to work. It's okay if you're like Pretti Patel and enjoy reading magazines and buying makeup all day," Leena said.

At the mention of Pretti, Rajput looked up sharply with an odd expression on his face.

"Who is Pretti Patel?" Mrs Gowda said.

"Pretti is Leena's school friend, they are very close," Rani said.

"It's good to have friends." She paused as if thinking. "Have I met this Pretti? Is she the grocer, you know old grocer Patel's girl? Have you met her Rajput?" Mrs Gowda asked, addressing to her son.

35

"She goes to the community centre, so we have met her there," Rajput said, looking away from his mother, pretending to take a sandwich from the tray on the small coffee table in front of him.

"Her name does sound familiar. I'm sure I have heard something about her." Mrs Gowda said, as she peered around at Roopa.

Rajput was now looking extremely uncomfortable and avoiding his mother's eyes.

"More tea? Leena pass round those sweetmeats and samosas," Rani said quickly; she knew something had happened in the room but she was not sure what it was. Why this sudden buzz about Pretti Patel? Pretti had been Leena's friend for as long as she could remember. 'Seems like an agreeable enough girl,' she thought.

Roopa deliberately took one of the samosas and looked up at Rani. "These are delicious Rani. Did you make them?"

"No, Leena did. She's a good cook."

"We must get together and swap some recipes, Leena, and then you can help me with the cooking," Mrs Gowda said.

"Yes, Mrs Gowda," Leena said softly, but she turned away and caught the eye of her brother who had been sitting listening to the conversation with interest. He winked at Leena who had trouble not laughing at the look on her brother's face.

"That would be good. You have to get to know each other before Leena moves in," Roopa said.

"What? We're going to live with you?" Leena exclaimed, and again Sevi pulled a face at Leena from the end of the sofa where he was hidden from view, at least as far as the visitors were concerned. Rani could see him and sent him a scathing look.

"Yes, Leena, then you can help me with the business paperwork and it will be more convenient for Rajput," Mrs Gowda said.

"I see," Leena said, a stony expression settling on her face. "I imagine it would be."

"What do you do in your job, Leena?" Mrs Gowda asked.

"Oh, you know, computer work, answering the phone, meeting clients and preparing legal papers, all that sort of thing," Leena replied distractedly.

Mr and Mrs Gowda exchanged a look and he turned to address Leena. "How long have you worked there, Leena?" Mr Gowda asked.

"About seven months since I left school. It's a good firm. But I am going to go ..."

"Well ... we will talk about that," he interrupted and then pointedly looked at Rajput. "Rajput may get you pregnant and then there will be no more need of this nonsense."

Rajput shrugged, as if it was a matter of little or no importance to him. Roopa exchanged a look with Rani and they both seemed very uncomfortable. There was a short awkward silence while they all drank more tea and munched on savouries. Rajput did not look up, or say anything more to Leena. Then after a few awkward minutes, Mr Gowda looked at his watch and got up from his chair.

"Well, I think it's time to go. We will be in touch regarding the wedding plans," Mr Gowda said. "Neela will let you know about the arrangements for the reception."

"Yes, that will be fine. I'll check that the local community centre is free on that date in July and we will get together to share the arrangements," Mr Purri replied.

"I'll be in touch with you, Mrs Purri, about catering and flowers and such. We have many connections you know," Mrs Gowda said.

"We will meet for coffee one morning next week?" Rani said. "Lion will start on the legal arrangements."

"Yes, that will be fine. Goodbye Leena, Sevi, and Mr and Mrs Purri. Are you coming Roopa?" Mrs Gowda asked. "We can give you a lift."

Roopa nodded her assent, she was not very happy, things had not gone well. The two young people seemed to actually dislike each other. "Yes, I'm coming," she muttered, glancing back at Leena who had not moved from the sofa, and was sitting staring vacantly in front of her.

"Oh, call me Rani please and my husband's name is Lion... after all we are going to be related," Rani said rather tensely.

"Speak to you next week then; I'll let my accountant know that you will be speaking to him about the settlement and such. Mrs Gowda, I mean Neela, will need to talk to Rani about the saris and all that paraphernalia. I'll leave that to the women," Mr Gowda said to Lion and laughed. "They love all that stuff. All we have to do is pay for it. Am I right, Lion?"

"Yes, Jemale," Lion replied.

"Goodbye then, see you all soon," Rajput said, before dashing out of the living room door with unnatural haste.

"Goodbye," Leena said watching the party go with some relief.

"Here's my card, Mr Purri, I mean Lion, we will be in touch," Mr Gowda said and handed Lion his business card. Reluctantly Leena arose from the coach and with Sevi followed the party to the front door.

"Goodbye Roopa, Goodbye Rajput," Rani said.

Rajput turned and waved his hand at Mrs Purri; then he turned and looked at Leena, a sad apologetic look on his face. "Goodbye Leena, it was good to meet you, I'm sorry if I was rude," he said quickly, before he turned and left the house.

After they left Lion went back into the living room and collapsed into his favourite chair, followed by Rani and Leena. They all looked completely drained.

"Well, that went well, I think?" Lion said, regarding his wife inquiringly.

"Hmmm," Leena replied, absentmindedly picking at her fingernails.

"Yes, he seems like a pleasant boy, got on well with Sevi," Rani said. "Stop that, Leena, you'll make them bleed."

Leena looked up at her mother, her face defiant.

"I don't want to marry him and especially in July when I will be going to university in September ..." Leena started to say.

"It's a good match; they are rich and he has useful connections," Lion said. "Why do you have to be so obstinate?"

Leena glared back at him, an angry expression on her face.

A meaningful glance went between Rani and Lion, and Rani moved to sit next to Leena. "I like him, he's polite and he's extremely good looking," Rani said. "What do you have against him, Leena?"

She leaned towards Leena and smiled, but it was a false smile and as she turned away towards her husband her face did not match her words. She looked very worried.

"I just don't like him, mum," Leena said, standing up and facing her father.

"You will get to know him and you will get to like him," Lion said. "These things take time."

"I want to go to university and have a career," she said standing rigidly, her hands going to her hips and her chin sticking out.

"We have talked about this, Leena," Lion said, his chin, too, was stuck out in that family trait of stubbornness.

"You have talked about this, you have not asked me. I do not want to marry Rajput Gowda, he is shallow and he is …" Leena said starting to cry.

"I like him, sis. I think he's cool," Sevi said.

"If you like him so much then why don't you marry him?" Leena said, and then she rushed from the room in tears, going upstairs to her room. Rani arose from the sofa to follow.

"No, Rani, let her cool down, she will be okay and come to her senses in time for the wedding," Lion said. "She is just being a stubborn girl."

"Oh Lion, she's so set against him," Rani said, looking down sadly at her husband.

"She will do as we decide. After all, we only want what it best for her, don't we? Jemale has some good contacts. A connection with that family can be extremely beneficial to all of us and to the business," Lion said. "Leena will comply with …"

"Oh Lion, are we doing the right thing?" Rani said.

"She'll come round, Rani. Now do we have any of those delicious pastries left?" he asked.

"Yes, I'll get them. Do you want some, Sevi?" Rani said as she got up to go into the kitchen. "Sevi …?"

"Yes, mum… thanks." Sevi gazed solemnly towards the front door; he turned and watched as his mother went into the kitchen. "Look dad, Leena's a clever girl. She should have the right to go to university if she wants."

"You should go to university. And not spend all your time playing computer games. Girls should get married and have children," Lion said emphatically, but even as he said it he looked embarrassed. "I mean, I …"

"Oh dad, you're so old-fashioned. Things are different these days... Leena should get an education."

Rani re-entered the room with a plate of sandwiches. Sevi took a plate full and then stood up to go back into the other room to resume his computer game, but he turned and confronted his father.

"For what it's worth, dad, I think Leena should go to university, she can get married when she has her education."

"Humph," Lion grunted.

"Sevi has a point, you know, and Leena is so clever; she always got top grades at school. I wish Sevi was doing half as well as she did," Rani said, "he can't seem to get his mind away from those silly computer games."

"Sevi will improve if he puts his mind to it; he's spoilt, and we should be stricter with him or he will waste his life away," Lion said reaching for the tray of the pastries and sandwiches.

"Yes, Lion," Rani agreed. But she was not really listening; the sound of the computer game had started up again in the front room.

Lion picked up a newspaper and munched on a samosa and Rani glanced up the stairs. There was a very worried expression in her eyes.

Chapter Nine

Yesterday was pure hell! Leena wrote in her diary.

She was sprawled on her bed, still wearing her panda print dressing grown over her pyjamas as she scribbled furiously. It was the Sunday morning after the ill-fated meeting with Rajput's parents.

Leena's diary (May 4th)

Well really!

Rajput and his pretentious mother and father. I felt like standing up and yelling at them… I don't want to marry your stupid son; he is a moron, an insipid, cultural wilderness, and a waste of space. I was so vex!

If only I could have done it, to see their faces. Mum would have been mortified and Dad – well, I'm so annoyed with my father – he is only thinking of himself – and the business opportunities that this marriage would bring. They say, "We only want what is best for you." What a load of crap! They are not thinking about me, only themselves. It's not bloody fair.

And that dress his mother wore; and Mum had made me wear my bloody sari.

I felt such an idiot. That dress must have cost over two hundred pounds, it was silk, and okay it was pretty, but – all the same she's such a snob, they both are.

They looked down their snooty noses at us, and Mum was running around like the Queen had come to tea. She's such a fronter *– that posturing cow and Rajput and his dad were nearly as bad. They hardly touched those stupid bloody sandwiches and the samosas and stuff we spent hours making. Not good enough for them I suppose?*

Rajput did not even talk to me; he was more interested in playing computer games with Sevi. When I think back he looked just as uncomfortable about the whole thing as me. I don't suppose he wants to get married either.

Perhaps I should try and talk to him, see if we can get things sorted. If we both refuse to get married they can't force us – can they? How can I get his phone number?

Leena jumped up from the bed and looked in her mobile phone and then in her address book.

It's not here, Mum and Dad will have it; no I can't ask them. I'm seeing Pretti today; she might have it or know someone who does.
Pretti has been acting very odd lately. I wonder what's up with her. She's quite secretive at times, like when she had a crush on that teacher. I hope she's not getting into something stupid again. She can be a bit vain and narrow minded at times, but I do love her and want to help if something is wrong. She has a good heart and has been a constant friend.

"Oh hell, Mum is calling me," Leena says to herself, "what does she want now? If it's some inane talk about saris, weddings and cooking curry, I will scream.

Chapter Ten

The windows of the new, silver Jaguar are steamed up. The car is in a secluded car park near the lake on the edge of the town. A couple can just be seen in the front seats, a man and a woman, who seem to be engaged in a very animated conversation.

The woman is crying and she scoops back her long dark hair, but her face is turned away from the man, who goes to put his arm around her shoulders. But she forcefully shrugs him away, moving over even farther in the seat until she is almost squashed up against the door. With eyes misty and full of tears she peers through the window, into the darkness of the empty car park.

"Please stop crying, baby; it's not my fault. Mum and Dad are set on it. They don't want to understand, that ..." Rajput puts his hand out towards the woman. "I don't love her. It's you that I want, you know that..." Rajput says. "You know that don't you baby?"

"You can't get married," the girl mumbles, her voice muffled by tears. "You can't."

"I don't want to, baby, I really don't want to. But they seem so set on it."

"She's my best friend," The girl breaks into even more violent sobs. "You just can't get married, especially to Leena."

"Baby please, don't cry, what can I do? It's not my fault," Rajput says, feeling very uncomfortable. He hates it when someone cries, and with this girl he feels so helpless. Why did his parents have to choose Leena to be his wife? He had tried to tell them that this arranged wedding business was so old-fashioned, but they just wouldn't listen.

"She doesn't want to marry you; you don't want to marry her. Oh, what a mess," the girl sobs. "It isn't fair... Stand up to them Raj. Can't you? I'll die if you marry her."

"I'll talk to my dad again; he will just have to understand." Rajput sighs. "Oh baby, do stop crying. We will work it out somehow. I can't bear to see you cry," he says again reaching out to hold her.

This time she allows him to put his arm around her but still jerks her face away towards the car window. Rajput groans and puts his face against her silky hair and inhales its jasmine fragrance; she always smells so good, he thinks. All his senses are stimulated, and he wants this girl so intensely that his body tingles.

"What can I do? I know, we can run away," he says. "They can't stop us getting together then."

The girl abruptly turns toward Rajput, her long hair falls forward obscuring her face, her eyes shine bright as she pushes her long lustrous mane aside.

"What? But how can we? My mum will go mad."

"If we run away, I can't get married to Leena and then we can come back when things have settled down and we can be together," Rajput says. "Then we can get married."

"Your mum and dad will never allow you to marry me. She hates me because of that gossip last year. But nothing happened." Pretti sobs. "I promise you, Raj, nothing happened."

"I know baby, I know." Rajput says. "But, we will get married."

"But your mum…"

"She doesn't know you like I do baby. She will love you when she gets to know you. Oh Pretti I love you. Baby, let's not fight," Rajput says pulling her towards him.

Rajput puts his hand up to her face and this time she turns towards him and willingly relaxes into his arms; he kisses her passionately and then moves his head back to gaze at her, he smooth's back her hair, caressing her face and neck.

"My beautiful girl, you always smell so good," he mutters and then his hand slides to her shoulder and down the front of her body until he holds her breast, through the pale blue, silky blouse.

"Oh Rajput, I do love you. But we shouldn't …" Pretti murmurs against his lips.

"It's okay, baby, we're almost engaged now. Come on… I love you so much and you're so gorgeous …" Rajput says, his raiding fingers opening her blouse, fumbling with the tiny mother-of-pearl buttons.

"Oh Rajput, oh baby oh…" Pretti moans as she pushes herself around in the car seat to lean towards him, "I love you so much."

"Me too, baby, me too," he gasps. "Shall we get in the back seat?"

"I don't know," Pretti says. "I'm still angry with you."

"It's not my fault, it's my parents…" he moans, his voice raspy with desire.

"But you went along with it; you went to her house and you met her parents!"

"It's okay, my baby girl, it's okay, we are going to be together. I promise… umm," Rajput says, his hand dropping to her knee, and slowly pulling up the soft material of her skirt.

"No," Pretti says pushing his hand away.

"Okay baby," Rajput says. He kisses her tenderly and his hand goes back to her open blouse. He now has one of her breasts free and is gently pinching its nipple between his thumb and forefinger, his head drops down to her neck and he kisses her, his lips leaving a trail of sensation down Pretti's throat. "Oh baby," he mutters, "I adore you."

"Raj," Pretti sighs, "Oh Raj, what are we to do?"

"We'll sort it out," he says against her breast. "Darling, we will be okay. Do you love me?"

"Yes, I love you, you know that I do."

"Then let's get into the back seat. I need you so bad."

"Okay," Pretti says. "But ...

"Now baby, I want you now," Rajput says urgently, then he leans past her and opens the car door, and they feel the cool evening air. They both clamber out of the car but before getting back in Pretti stands and looks out over the Kent countryside. It is a beautiful evening and the last rays of the setting sun are just disappearing below the horizon, then she turns to Rajput. Her light summer skirt flows around her legs as she twists towards him, caught by the breeze of the mild spring evening.

"Oh Rajput, I love you so much," Pretti sighs. "It will be okay, won't it? It'll be okay?"

"Sure it will baby. Now, let's not talk anymore." Rajput says as he walks to her side of the vehicle and he takes her hand and helps her, eagerly, into the back seat of the Jaguar. They kiss again and immediately Rajput starts to push up the hem of Pretti's skirt, his hand moving relentlessly upwards.

"But Raj, we shouldn't."
"Please baby, I need you so bad."
"Oh. Raj darling, I do love you."
"I know baby, I know, and we will be together, but let us…"
"We will be together. Your parents can't stop us…"

Then Pretti sighs as Rajput kisses her breast, again pulling aside the cup of her bra, his hands roaming over her body, one gliding over her hip and down to her knee and again he pushes up her skirt his hand going higher and higher up her thigh.

"Baby," he mumbles. "Oh baby, I need you."
"Raj," Pretti says. "What about Leena?"
"Forget Leena, she doesn't want to marry me. She wants to go to university."
"I know but…" He stops her mouth with a kiss.
"Put your leg ... That's it baby I can't wait. Oh that's wonderful, oh my darling Pretti."
"Raj," Pretti moans as she submits to Rajput's passionate advances.

Then there is silence, just the sighs and moans from the back seat, within the cocoon of the dark silvery Jaguar. Soft cries are punctuating the night air as an owl hoots in the distance and gradually all colour fades from the velvety, dark blue night sky.

Chapter Eleven

"You're going to be late if you don't get moving," Rani said to her son, who was just coming down the stairs. "I have made you some sandwiches."

"I hope they're not left over from Saturday?" he asked.

"No, they are fresh, but I have put in a couple of samosas, they're still okay, and you have a banana and some crisps."

"Mum, where's my gym kit?"

"On the sideboard next to the window in your room," Rani replied, "where I always leave it."

"Thanks and my trainers?"

"And your trainers are at the bottom of the stairs."

Sevi rushed back up the stairs and came down stuffing shorts and tee-shirt into his school bag. At that moment the doorbell rang and Jim shouted out. Rani opened the door as Jim was just about to give the bell another press.

"Morning Mrs P," Jim said.

"Hello Jim, how are your mum and dad?"

"Okay. Hello Sevi, you coming?"

"Gotta go mum, see you later," Sevi said. "Bye."

"Goodbye boys."

Sevi grabbed his trainers and dashed out the door. Rani went out to the porch to watch as the two boys headed off down the road. She stayed for a few minutes and observed as they disappeared around the corner, then looked up at the sky and shuddered.

"Looks like rain," she said to herself, "and Leena did not take her umbrella. I hope that girl is okay."

Leena had not spoken to her parents all day Sunday and had left the house early Monday morning, looking sad and subdued.

Rani closed the door and sighed. "I hope we are doing the right thing. That boy didn't seem very interested in my beautiful girl. She deserves a good man, one who will love and cherish her."

Chapter Twelve

"What's this about your sister getting married?" Jim said as they walked along the road. "My mum said that she heard Leena arguing about it in the garden the other day."

"Yes, Dad is set on it, but poor Leena, she's very *vex*, and well, she hates the guy," Sevi replied. "Anyway she should go off to university like she wants. She is a bright girl, much cleverer than me."

"That wouldn't be hard, Sevi," Jim joked.

"Hey, watch it mate."

"No offence, it's like me and my sister. Dawn is the clever one, but I try, you gotta try, keeps the oldies off your back." Jim paused. "Mum is always on at us, 'you want to get somewhere in life,' she says. 'Don't end up like your dad.' She's always on his case, I feel quite sorry for him sometimes."

It was a dull overcast day, but because the boys were chatting they hardly noticed the weather. They had become good friends in the four years since the Price family had moved in next door. They enjoyed each other's company, playing football, computer games and even doing homework together.

"My mum and dad don't argue much. Dad just tells Mum what he wants and that's it. Leena is different; she wants her own life. It's hard for us, you know."

"Hard?" Jim queried. "What do you mean?"

"Yes, well, they, my parents that is, are used to a different culture, whereas we're trying to live in … well, with two cultures. Know what I mean?"

"Yes, I think so."

"And it is easier for boys," Sevi said. "But don't tell my sister I said that."

"I see what you mean, but boys always have more freedom, don't they? And women have often had a raw deal of it throughout history.

Did you hear about this thing that's happening in Egypt, India and other countries?"

"No. What thing?" Sevi asked.

"It's called 'Tormenting Eve'; gangs of men taunt and even attack women on the streets. In Egypt young women have even been stripped and sexually assaulted by crowds of rampaging men."

"How awful, but why?" Sevi asked. "Oh yes, there was that case of that girl being raped in Delhi."

"Dad says it's a primitive thing; people always take their frustration out on the weaker person and in these cases women are feeling the brunt of it."

"That's terrible. People can be so cruel and so stupid." Sevi sighed. "Do you ever feel like you have no control, that the things that happen just don't make any sense?"

"All the time, mate."

"I do wonder what goes on in people's heads at times," Sevi said. "Leena gets very upset about these things. She really cares about the environment and the state of people's lives in the world."

"Yes, I know it's strange world." Jim shrugged. "What's that saying something about - that the madmen are in charge or something? Oh I can't remember. It's a mad world."

"It sure is."

The boys walked on in silence for a few minutes.

"I'd say that my mum was the boss in my house," Jim said. "Poor Dad, he gets a right earful at times. Mum has a terrible temper."

"I like your dad, and Dawn, but your mum is scary at times." Sevi laughed. "Is that why you come over to ours when they're having a row?"

"You bet," Jim replied, "specially now with Dad out of work again."

The Prices had had some hard times over the years and there had been many arguments between his parents, which meant that Jim was often glad to escape the house and go off somewhere with Sevi.

"Dawn and Dad are very close. Mum bullies him a bit, but Dawn stands up to her," Jim said. "I will ask Dawn to talk to Leena and find out what is happening with this wedding business. Do you know him? I mean, the boy they want her to marry."

"Yes. His name is Rajput Gowda. I like him, he's into computer games and stuff, but even I can see that he's not right for Leena. She's much more serious and academic, and he is a bit ... well, shallow for her. I think she should go to university and get her degree. Time enough for marriage when she gets older, I reckon," Sevi said soberly. "Makes you wonder how the right people get together. Don't it?"

"Year, take my oldies, I love them both but there are times I wonder what my dad was thinking."

"Your dad," Sevi paused, "he seems like a nice bloke. Your mum scares me, she always looks so ... well sour ... she always looks like she has swallowed a lemon or something, *in' it*."

"She is bitter, and she's always on at Dad. He can't help it if he can't find any work, I know he tries."

"It's my dad that goes on at me, get some education, do your homework, make something of your life. He goes on and on." Sevi paused and then asked. "Why can't your dad find work? He's intelligent, highly qualified. I know it's hard. I do worry sometimes what there will be available when we leave school. What do you want to do Jim, college or university?"

"I think my dad has just been unlucky. But I am sure something will turn up soon. I don't know what I want to do. Play football. Maybe go to sports-college," Jim said. "What about you?"

"I want to do something with computers, maybe programming or something. I will probably go on to college. That's what the parents want, *in' it?*"

"We have to keep the oldies happy, don't we," Jim laughed and punched Sevi on the arm.

"Hey," Sevi yelped, "watch it, that hurt."

"Sorry mate, I forgot you were so delicate."

"I'll give you delicate," Sevi said. "You wait until the football match Saturday; we'll see who is fragile then."

"Yes Sevi. Just don't forget that we are on the same side?"

"Okay," Jim said. "Do you think we will win?"

"Course we will," Sevi replied. "Are the girls coming to watch?"

"I hope so," Jim replied. "I like Dawn's friends especially your sister Leena, although Linda is a bit of a skeet."

"What's a *skeet*?" Sevi queried.

"A *skeet* is a female 'chav'. Someone pretending to be something they're not," Jim explained.

"Not heard that one," Sevi said. "She's pretty though. So is Pretti."

"I guess." Jim turned and smiled at Sevi, "But not too bright."

"How so?"

"Well, the other day when Pretti was visiting Dawn, Dad and I were talking about football…"

"Well, girls don't know much about football, do they?

"No, but listen, this is funny." Jim said. "Dad was complaining about some Italian footballer who had been arrested for throwing matches," Jim said.

"I heard about that," Sevi replied.

"Yes. Well, Pretti overheard and then my father asked her what she thought." Jim laughed. "She said, 'Oh yes. Actually, I think it's all very petty. I know it's a thuggish way to behave, but as long as they didn't actually set light to anyone, I don't see what all the fuss is about," My dad looked at me, and I burst out laughing. 'What,' Pretti said and then she marched off in a huff."

"That's a classic," Sevi replied. "Here we are." They had reached the school gates.

At that moment the boys saw several of their school mates and entered the playground just as the bell went for the first classes.

"See you at lunch," Sevi said.

"Yes, mate," Jim said, "see you laters, *in' it*. There's my *crew*."

"Laters," Sevi replied and turned towards his classroom.

"I still think she's lovely," Jim yelled, as he dashed off to greet his friends.

Part Two

Chapter Thirteen

"What hall is it, Leena?" Rani asked. "Look, there's a sign. It says the University of Brighton, halls of residence."

"It's called Byron Hall. Mum, look," Leena replied. "There it is over there."

Leena pointed to a red brick building across the road. Mr Purri stopped the car outside and they all piled out. He began to pull a huge case out of the boot. Leena and Sevi also had bundles of carrier bags and Mrs Purri was carrying a large yellow cool bag. It was late September.

"Well, let's get this suitcase in, it weighs a ton." Lion staggered under the weight. "Give me a hand, Sevi, will you?"

"I can manage from here. You don't all have to come in," Leena said.

"Don't be ridiculous Leena, you can't carry all this," Sevi replied, taking one end of the massive case. "What have you got in here?"

"Come on, let's get this stuff inside," Lion said.

"I want to see where my girl is going to live. We'll not leave you here alone, don't be daft, girl." Rani grabbed a carrier bag in her other hand.

They trudged off across the grass towards the halls of residence then climbed up the stairs until they found room 202 on the second floor.

"You would never have managed this on your own," Rani panted as she reached the top of the stairs.

"Whatever have you got in this case?" Sevi muttered as he dropped it down outside the door.

The door to the room was open and Leena walked in, tentatively shadowed by her mum and dad. Sevi followed, dragging the large case.

"Just clothes, books and stuff," Leena replied. "Is someone there?"

When they entered the room they found a pretty, young woman with pale, reddish blonde hair standing in the middle of the room; she was surrounded by cases, clothes and boxes of books. The L shaped room was divided into two parts; the bedroom and then a study area and a small bathroom.

"Hello there," Leena addressed the slim, fair girl, who looked around at them in surprise. "Are you my room-mate?"

"Hi. I'm Jane Bond. Call me Janie." Then she looked down at her feet and surveyed the mess. "I don't know where to start."

"Hi. I'm Leena Purri, and this is my family, my brother, Sevi, and my parents, Rani and Lion." Leena smiled at the look of dismay on the girl's face.

"Hello. Pleased to meet you. I've just arrived myself, so please excuse the mess. Which side do you want?"

"What?" Leena said.

"Which side, by the wall or by the window? I don't mind." Janie indicated the two beds.

"Wall," Leena said, dropping her bags onto the bed. "Phew. I didn't know I had so much stuff."

"Fine, that's settled then." Janie pushed a box of books over towards the second bed and pulled a case up on to it, flipping it open and starting to sort out the contents.

"Where's the fridge?" Rani asked as she looked around the room.

"There's no fridge in the room, but there's a kitchen next door. But I wouldn't put anything in it if I were you, because it's sure to get nicked," Janie replied.

"My mum has sent along some provisions, should keep me going till spring." Leena laughed at the look on her mum's face. "Do you like Indian food, Janie?"

Rani looked indignant, but started to empty out masses of plastic containers from the cool bag and put them on the table.

"I don't want you starving yourself, Leena. We'll have to buy her a small fridge for the room, Lion." Rani turned to her husband. "The room's not bad, I like the colour scheme. I would never have thought of putting blue and green together like that, but it sort of works."

The room was painted a pale blue, the curtains and bedspreads were blue and green stripes with amber and gold flecks in the material. It all looked very comfortable; there were two chairs, two chests of drawers and two wardrobes. A central light hung over the compact study area on the opposite wall and there were lamps on the night tables next to the beds.

"Yes, it's lovely." Leena peeped into the bathroom then pulled a face at her mum and turned to Janie. "Do I look starved?" Leena stood with her hands on her hips and laughed.
"No, you look great, and if you want any help disposing of the food, I'm your girl. No task too big for Janie Bond," Janie quipped.
They laughed and Sevi smiled at Janie. From his body language he seemed to have taken quite a liking to Leena's new room-mate.
"I think it's a cool name," he said smiling at Janie shyly, "Janie Bond."
"I bet you get teased about your name?" Leena said.
"Not so you'd notice. I don't know what my mum was thinking. Though, I do know that she had read a lot of Ian Fleming novels and that she really wanted a boy. I do try to live up to the name in my own way." There was a pause while Janie looked down at the mess surrounding her. All she had managed to do was transfer the contents of her case into a jumbled heap on her bed. "Look, I have to go and see someone, get some milk and such; ignore my gear and make yourselves at home. I'll tidy my kit away when I get back."
"Thanks Janie, see you later," Leena said. "You don't have to leave on our account."
"Yes, I know ... See you later, nice to meet you, Sevi, Mr and Mrs Purri. I will keep an eye on your girl here and show her where everything is. Do you have your book list yet Leena?" she asked. Janie seemed rather hyper and excited and did appear to be acting a bit erratically.

"No, and I have to get registered and collect my course material tomorrow," Leena replied.

"Me too. Well, I have some stuff but I still have to join the union and do a few things. We can go together if you like. There's a great library here and lots of things going on. I'm quite excited, as you can tell." Janie smiled. "Do you want anything from the shop?"

"No thanks, I think Mum has supplied me with everything I need for the duration." Leena's mum looked offended again, but Leena turned and gave her a big smile. "I'm extremely grateful Mum, save me worrying about shopping for a few days, anyway."

"See *yer* then." Janie grabbed her jacket and bag and left the room. The Purri family stood and looked at each other uneasily.

"Seems like a nice girl, if a bit jumpy?" Rani said looking after Janie, "I hope they haven't put you in with some junkie. Okay, where do you want these things, Leena?"

"Mum, how can you say such things?" Leena looked shocked, as she turned to gaze at her mum.

"Don't go getting into the wrong company. I understand there are a lot of strange people living in Brighton," Lion said. "It has a reputation for gays and such."

"There are a lot of strange people living everywhere these days. Now look, I can unpack by myself, why don't you get going? Anyway, I will be too busy studying to get into too much mischief." Leena turned and winked at Sevi without her parents seeing.

Sevi laughed and went over to the window.

"I like her. She's very pretty in a flaky sort of way." Sevi was looking out the window, but he turned to Leena. "You got a nice view from here, sis. But I bet it's…"

"Oh, Leena, my baby girl, leaving home; to live in some strange place. I can't believe it. You should be married now. How could they? Your own friend," Rani interrupted and started to sniff, taking a handkerchief out of her pocket and dabbing her eyes.

"Come on now, Rani, we have been over this. The boy was not good enough for our Leena," Lion said. "We will find someone better."

"But to run off like that, and with Pretti, that sly little bitch," Rani started to say.

"Not now, Rani, and in front of Sevi, and we have all had enough of ... let's just look to the future and how proud Leena is going to make us when she gets a university degree. We can only hope that Sevi pulls his finger out and starts to show some promise," Lion said taking his wife's arm.

Sevi and Leena exchanged a grin, unseen by their parents and Leena walked over to look out of the window next to Sevi.

"You're my spy," Leena whispered. "You must let me know what's happening back home. Email me with any news. Okay?"

"Sure thing, sis, I still can't believe he ran off with Pretti," Sevi whispered back.

"What are you two whispering about?" Rani looked over at them suspiciously.

"I admit things have not worked out how we planned, but let's make the best of it," Lion said. "Leena is at university, as she wanted, and there is plenty of time to find a more suitable boy for her when she has graduated."

Leena turned to face her father. "Dad, I don't want to get married."

"But Leena, you will, you will. Why, when I think of it..." Rani said still trying to hold back the tears.

"Enough, Rani, we'll leave Leena to her unpacking. Brighton is not that far away, we'll see her often," Lion said. "I think we should leave her to settle in. We can go and buy a small fridge, come on now. Come Rani. You too, Sevi, let's leave Leena and come back when we have the fridge." Lion turned to his daughter, a sad look in his eyes. "We do love you, Leena; be good and make us proud."

"My little girl..." Rani murmured, as her husband led her towards the door.

"No more tears, Mum, you promised." Leena darted forward and hugged her mother at the door. "Bye now. I'll see you later and I will come for the weekend at the end of the month."

"Bye sis, be good," Sevi said and laughed.

"Bye Mum, bye Dad, and you too, Sevi, you be good," Leena said. "You don't really need to worry about the fridge, dad ..." They all embraced and Rani and Sevi left the room but Lion held back.

"It's no big deal, Leena, your mum will be happier if she knows you have your own food. Let's humour her on this, okay?" Lion said. "She is losing her precious little girl."

"Okay Dad. See you in a *mo*," Leena kissed her father on the cheek.

She was left standing in the room surrounded by bags, cases and books. She smiled, and then started to laugh. She threw her arms wide, spun around and flung herself on to the bed with a look of pure joy on her face. After a few seconds, she got up.

"Thank you, Pretti. Thank you very much," she muttered chuckling to herself. "I can't believe I didn't know." Then she laughed again. "What have you left me to eat, mum, suddenly I am ravenously hungry. I will miss your cooking, if not the nagging."

Leena peered into the cool bag and took out a plastic tray full of Indian delicacies and started to eat an onion bargee. "Yummy," Leena mumbled. There was also a carton of chocolate milk, which she promptly opened and started to drink.

"Chocolate milk, my favourite, oh mum, you're a star. I will miss you all."

She then started to unpack her bags and hang things in the cupboards and put her books on the shelf next to her bed.

"I'm going to like it here," she said. "I just know it."

Chapter Fourteen

As Leena walked across the grass at the university campus on Monday morning she saw Janie standing talking to two boys. Leena had just been to her course induction class and she was carrying an armful of folders. She immediately walked over to them looking with interest at Janie's companions.

"Hi there," Leena said interrupting their conversation. "Sorry to butt in."

"Hi," Janie replied as she turned to greet her new friend with a smile. "No problem."

"I've just got my book lists for economics, there's so much to get," Leena said.

"Get them second-hand. What course are you doing?" One of the boys asked eyeing Leena speculatively.

"Me. I'm taking social economics," Leena replied, "and third world technology studies."

Leena looked hard at the boy who had addressed her and then turned to Janie with an enquiring lift of her eyebrow.

"Sorry, let me introduce you. Leena, this is Alum Contem and Pieter Pieterson. Alum and Pieter, this is Leena Purri, my roommate."

"Pleased to meet you, Leena," Alum said giving Leena a long appraising look before turning back to Janie.

"Hi there, welcome to the mad house," Pieter said. "I'm studying economics as well, with science and third world technology. The book list is scary but you can get most of it from the library and there is a great second-hand book shop in Brighton that's really cheap. I'll show you if you like." Pieter gazed with interest at Leena.

"You'll soon find your way around," Alum said. "We'll all be finding our way…"

"Just let me know if there's anything you need help with," Pieter interrupted, and moved closer to Leena. "Maybe we could …"

Alum looked at his friend in amusement.

"Down boy," Janie said. "Leena is here to study; she's not going to be interested in you, so spread your Nordic charm elsewhere."

Pieter paused and gave Janie a sidewise glance then he looked back at Leena with a captivated expression on his face.

"Where are you from Leena? London?" Alum asked.

Alum was six foot two, well-built with wide shoulders. He was wearing cream chinos, a pale blue denim shirt and a black jacket.

"I'm from Tonbridge in Kent," Leena replied, looking from Pieter to Alum with interest. "What about you? What are you studying?"

"London, near Harrow, do you know it? I'm taking economics, science and technology. Like you but not so green," Alum said flashing his almond shaped eyes so that they crinkled at the corners. He had a sardonic look about him, as if he did not take very much in life seriously.

"What do you mean 'green'?" Leena asked studying the tall Asian boy with interest.

"Social economics, that includes all that tree-hugging liberal stuff, full of greenies, doesn't it?" he said.

"I do care about the environment, if that's what you mean." Leena regarded Alum coolly as she shuffled her folders.

"He's just teasing you, don't take any notice," Janie said.

"Oh," Leena said and looked away, embarrassed at how he had so easily provoked her. "Well, I must go. See you later, Janie. Are you going to that environmental talk later? That guy from Friends of the Earth is coming."

"Yes, but I have to go to the library first, want to come?"

"I'm on my way there now. Okay, see you in a minute," Leena said then she turned and walked away towards the library. As she went she looked back at the three of them, Pieter and Alum were both staring after her.

"Bye Leena, be seeing you," Pieter said.

"Take care, Greenie," Alum shouted.

"Pretty girl that," observed Pieter.

"Not my type, a bit too serious," Alum said indifferently.

"What's your type then?" Pieter said laughing.

"Someone ... less serious," Alum said.

"She's very serious and she works hard, but she's fun too," Janie said. "So you take it easy on her, do you hear?"

"Works hard? We only just got here," Alum said.
"I know but ... Leena has already done a lot of reading."
"Crikey," Pieter said. "She is serious!"
"Yes, come on, it's time for our induction class, Casanova," Alum said. Pieter made a fake punch at Alum then they both laughed and said goodbye to Janie.
"Take care, Janie, see you tonight," Alum said.
"Yes. See you Janie," Pieter said.
"Bye, see you both later," Janie said.

As Alum and Pieter headed off towards the university building for their class, Janie watched them leave with a wistful look on her face. Then she shrugged and ran to catch up with Leena. Pieter, in contrast to Alum, was slim and blond. He had a lean build and was slightly stooped under his baggy jumper and blue jeans. But his eyes were bright blue and sparkled in his long pale face as he turned and watched the girls disappear towards the library.

"Gosh, she's gorgeous," Pieter said.
"Yes and the Indian girl's not bad either," Alum answered with a chuckle.
"I meant Leena," Pieter said, turning his gaze to Alum who grinned at him mercilessly. "She's stunning."
"I know you did. Look mate; don't turn your dizzy, blond head for that one; she will not be interested in you." Alum shrugged. "I've met her type before; she has a lot to prove, probably escaped some arranged wedding or something to be here. She's going to have to put all her efforts into proving herself to the family."
"Really?" Pieter asked. "But she seems ..."
"Yes, really," Alum answered. "But we can have some fun with those two, they are both gorgeous girls and I think they will be good company."
"Do you fancy her?" Pieter asked.
"Who? Janie?"
"No. Leena, for heaven's sake, Alum, are you being deliberately contrary?" Pieter said in exasperation.
"Yes, it's such fun to tease you," Alum smirked. "I think Leena will be a good victim to the tease. This is going to be fun."

"You should have more consideration for people; this is a challenging time … for people."

"Yes, old friend. I'm sorry, I will be more considerate," Alum said contritely.

"I'll believe that when I see it."

"Oh come on, you must admit that we will need to have a bit of fun to get through the next three years." Alum was gazing off towards the main lecture rooms where a crowd of students was now gathering. "Look, the student union bar is open let's go over and investigate, after this induction."

"Righty-oh," Pieter said, and with one last look towards the library the two boys headed off into the main building.

Chapter Fifteen

Leena and Janie hit it off straight away and it was Janie's blasé manner that helped Leena to cope with the first few months of being away from home. At first it was a relief to be away from the nagging and continual recriminations from her parents over the 'not to be arranged wedding' but then after a while she missed her friends, Sevi and even Mum and Dad. Sevi e-mailed nearly every day with all the gossip about Pretti and Rajput and what was going on in the street with her friends. Leena also spoke to her Mum and Dad on the phone every few days.

Leena's diary (1st November)

I've just spoken to Mum on the phone, good heavens; you would think I was in Outer Mongolia and not an hour away in the car.

Are you eating properly? You're not staying out all night, meeting boys, going to parties, taking drugs, having sex? Well she didn't actually ask that but the 'have you met any boys' question was loaded with the sex issue. She doesn't seem to realise just how much work we have to do, no time to have fun. Well not much anyway.

I didn't tell her about Alum and Pieter, who we do see quite a lot of, but we are working on projects together and they're friends of Janie and now friends of mine.

I like them both very much, but Alum can be very confrontational. Pieter is lovely but follows Alum around like a big puppy dog. And I sometimes catch him watching me, which can be a bit disconcerting at times! I think he finds me interesting or something!

Janie says that he fancies me but I hardly believe that can be true.

I asked Janie about it but she wouldn't say anything that made any sense.

'My heart is hungry for love,' she said. 'Well. The main difference between a man and a woman is that the man always puts his stomach before his heart and a woman does the opposite.'

I asked her what that meant and she replied. 'I have no idea; it was something my mother used to say.'

I asked Janie how they met – Alum and Pieter that is.

She told me that Pieter was in London with his parents as a child; his father is something to do with the Danish Embassy and was assigned to London for several years. Pieter met Alum at school and they hit it off, both being new to the area and the odd ones out at the school so to speak.

Janie met Pieter via an old school friend Lydia, who was living in Ealing and she found out that he was going to the University of Brighton. Lydia was also supposed to be going to Brighton but changed to Bristol at the last moment for some reason. I can't remember why, something to do with a boyfriend going there from what I can tell. Men really muck up our lives at times.

Talking of men, Mum and Dad are still rattling on about an arranged wedding. I do hope they forget the idea and give me some peace. Sevi tells me that Mum still goes on about Pretti and Rajput all the time, and how they let me down. And my father is constantly lamenting the business opportunities that he is missing out on, which only confirms to me that they were not thinking of my happiness but what a great contact Mr Jemale would have been.

Hey ho, well I had better get on with some work. I have two essays to do and I want to do some ground work for the debate tonight. It can go towards my end of year environmental stability project. Janie will be back from her class soon and she will want to talk. She talks a lot about Pieter, I wonder if she fancies him. No, I think she likes Alum or maybe that other boy Eggs. What a strange name, I must ask Janie about it. Who knows, she really does not say. I think she has a secret and she hardly ever talks about her family.

Anyway back to my books.

Chapter Sixteen

It is now several months into term and Janie and Leena have become very involved with the university program, including some of the environmental debates that proliferated in the university common rooms.

"Here it is," one of the students said, as he pushed past Janie and entered the room letting the door shut in their faces.
"Hey," Janie said.
"Sorry," the boy remarked. "I'm late."
"So are we," Eggs answered. "Is this the right room?"
"Yes, there's a poster, look."
There was a poster on the door saying: 'Debate on economic policy for renewable energy in rural Africa. Discuss.'
"Right, let's go in, Janie."
Eggs shoved into the room and held the door open for Janie.
"Yes. This is the room," Janie said looking around, "and it sounds like it's started already."
"Sure has," Eggs said.
When Janie and Eggs entered the debating room the dialogue was going at full steam. Eggs real name was Benedict, Benedict Pinkerton, but everybody called him Eggs.
"Yes, look," Janie said, "and Leena and the boys are here already."

In fact, quite a heated argument was underway. Leena, Pieter, Alum and several other students were seated in a circle. Leena suddenly stood up and began talking animatedly, her face flushed in frustration as she addressed Alum, who sat, one leg casually crossed over the knee of other, as he lounged back in his seat, an amused and intent expression on his face. Leena was oblivious to anything except her argument with Alum.

"Given up-to-date technology these communities can be independent. Solar power is cost-effective and easy to install and can give a community the amenities they need to become self-sufficient, as well as up to date in new technology," Leena said passionately. "Can't you see that fuel and water are what every community needs to survive and with renewable ..."

"Yes, they do need modern technology, but at what cost, and is renewable energy the answer?" Alum interrupted. "These cultures have survived thousands of years without any ..."

"There are agencies that can help. These communities have always used renewable energy; they've had to gather fuel, animal dung, for example," Leena said, ignoring Alum's last comment.

"Yes, and the World Bank and charities like OXFAM will supply small loans to get them started," Pieter interjected. "This gives them a sustainable resource..."

"Yes. The West supplies the finance but what do we get in return. A dependent nation, reliant on technology they can't afford to keep up," said Alum interrupting Pieter.

"But, they can't just be left to starve, when modern technology would make all the difference," Leena said angrily.

"It's nature's own way of controlling the population," Alum said, deliberately goading Leena.

"What absolute rubbish." Leena sat down abruptly and glared at Alum. "So you think it's alright for women to walk six miles a day just to get fresh water, and that children die because they are given dried milk that it is mixed with dirty water and that thousands die every year of AIDS when the drugs that could save them are withheld?" Leena was getting heated. She then turned her gaze to Pieter and gave him a beseeching look, "Pieter?"

"No, I don't. I think we have a responsibility to help. But..." Pieter said, eyeing Leena expectantly.

"That's all very well, but we can't just dole out aid indefinitely; let the people take out loans, and be responsible for them," Alum cut in.

"Then they end up in debt and forget how to feed their children in the traditional ways. They become reliant on imported foods," Leena continued. "Did you know that when Uganda was in the middle of the biggest ever famine they were still exporting food to the West?"

"And buying armaments," Eggs added.

"Now you're just being emotive and sentimental. It's a hard world out there and communities have to develop at their own pace," Alum said, ignoring Egg's comment.

"Here we go again," said Janie, as she and Eggs settled themselves on two chairs just outside the main group.

"Come on you two. Let's play nicely," Pieter said. "We all know that there are two sides to this debate."

"Tell that to Alum, he is the one being insensitive," Leena said, flashing her eyes at Pieter.

"Come on now, Greenie. I didn't mean to be inconsiderate," Alum said contritely, but turning and winking at Janie. "Hi you two, what were you saying, Eggs?"

"Alum has a point, but maybe we should concentrate on reducing population in these areas," Eggs said. "Also there are countries like India who until recently were receiving vast amounts of foreign aid, but have some of the richest citizens in the world, and are spending millions of pounds on a space programme. And their population is growing and growing and more and more people are living on the streets or in slums with no fresh water or basic facilities."

Eggs was an intense, tall, good-looking boy with green eyes and fair hair. Only his mother called him Benedict. Or his father, when he was in trouble, then it was always: "Benedict, where are you, boy?" He had a scar on his right eyebrow from a fall when he was a child, which gave him a rakish look. He was in the same hall of residence as Pieter and they had become good friends.

"That's true, Eggs, but it's not population that's the main problem it's the greed and corruption of the local governments and in Africa the never-ending wars that eat up all the money and …." Pieter started to say.

"And that means there is not enough money left to fund these environmental and humanitarian schemes except from foreign aid and charities, and that the ordinary people don't benefit," Eggs replied.

"Yes, but is cheap energy the answer? It only makes the foreign suppliers and contractors rich," Alum said. "Countries like China are buying up vast tracts of land and taking over water supplies…"

"Okay, I agree people are getting rich on the back of these technologies," Leena interrupted, "but you must agree that renewable energy has to be the answer. We can't have Third World nations building atomic power stations. They don't have oil or coal but they do have wind and plenty of sunshine."

"Renewable energy has to be the answer; the question is how to pay for it. The main problem is water. The entire world is facing a water shortage. The next wars will be about water not fuel, believe me," Pieter said, "water and food."

"That's so true," one of the other students added. "In a NATO report they called water 'Blue Gold' and said that the world was in danger of a water shortage."

Alum was ignoring Pieter and the other students and concentrating on Leena.

"Yes, I concede that renewables are the most suitable solution, for out of the way rural situations, as long as the local people are trained in these technologies and able to manufacture the spares they will need when things need maintaining…" Alum said smiling tentatively at Leena. "But …"

"Good, that's decided then. I have to go, got an essay to write and a tutorial in five minutes," Leena said looking at her watch and then she turned her head and noticed Janie and Eggs. "Hi Janie, Eggs. I didn't notice you come in. See you later."

Leena got up and left the room and as she passed through the door she turned and looked back and smiled cheekily at Alum. "See you tomorrow," she said.

"What tutorial is at this time of night?" Alum said looking confusedly at the closing door. "She's so annoying."

Several of the students started to pack up their books and drift out of the room but Pieter and Alum held back.

"You do wind each other up," Pieter said. "Why do you do that?"

"Yes, I know, but it's so much fun to get her all riled up, she looks so animated and flushed and lovely, I just can't resist it," Alum replied.

"You like her, don't you?" Pieter asked.

"Of course I do, she's fun and gorgeous, and well, fun."

"No, I mean you like her." Pieter turned away to collect his jacket.

Alum looked up with a startled expression on his face. Then he shrugged.

"Yes, well no. No, I don't think of her like that," he said gathering his books and swinging his pack up on to his back. "Let's go, I have some reading to do for tomorrow."

As they left the room Pieter looked apprehensive; he again looked furtively at Alum and started to speak, then stopped and turned to Janie and Eggs.

"Coming to the Student Union, Pieter?" Janie asked.

"Yes, why not." But then Pieter twisted around to wait for Alum. "So ... so you wouldn't mind ... it would be okay if I made a play for her?" he whispered. "I think she's great..."

"You go for it. Good luck to you. Of course, you don't stand a chance," Alum said quietly, with a shrug. "You know that."

"I might just do that. I know the odds are against me, but a guy's got to try..."

Pieter strode ahead and joined Janie and Eggs. Alum followed, his face set in an uncertain smile. He shrugged again and watched Pieter walking off down the corridor.

"He ain't got *no chance*," Alum mumbled to himself. "In any case what do I care?" But the look on his face contradicted his words.

"Where is Leena off to in such a hurry?" Eggs asked.

"I think she has a tutorial with Professor Clarke, something to do with her dissertation on the viability of solar power in India or something," Janie said.

"She's very keen, isn't she?" Eggs said.

"I think she has a lot to prove, her parents didn't really want her to come to university," Janie said, "and she's determined to do well."

"I don't think there is any doubt that she will do well, she's so focused," Eggs said. "But she gets so wound up and Alum seems to taunt her."

"He does it on purpose," Pieter said from behind them. "Gosh, I'm hungry."

"One can be too serious," Eggs responded.

"Yes. She must take some time to have fun," Pieter said. "You can't work all the time, can you, Janie?"

"Well Pieter, that is certainly true in your case," Janie laughed. "Let's go for a drink. Are you coming, Alum?"

"No Janie," Alum said. He had appeared behind Pieter, with a perturbed and distracted look about him. "I have this essay to finish for tomorrow; see you in the morning."

Alum sauntered off, his shoulders low and his head forward as he disappeared down the corridor towards the main doors of the building.

"I think I'll be off as well," Pieter said. And he left via the main entrance; his eyes followed Alum as walked away towards the town. Pieter waved Janie and Eggs a quick goodbye and strode off towards the halls of residence.

Janie watched his back and then turned to Eggs. "What's got into him? He never usually says no to a visit to the student bar."

"It looks like it's just you and me then," Eggs said. "Those two obviously have something on their minds."

"Okay," Janie said with one last wistful glance at the disappearing Pieter before taking Eggs' arm and heading for the bar. "Let's go."

Chapter Seventeen

Leena's diary (February 28th)

Well, I'll be! Sevi has just emailed me to say that Pretti has had a baby, apparently they went up to Gretna Green and got married and then she fell pregnant and are now back in Tonbridge with Rajput's family. Pretti pregnant! I just can't imagine it. She was always so fussy about her figure and her hair and such like. I wonder if she took out her belly ring before the birth, I think she must have.

I would have liked to be a fly on the wall when they arrived at his mum and dad's house with a bun in the oven. Wow. I've told Sevi that he has got to find out all the details.

We were such good friends, I do wish her the best; she did do me a huge favour running away with Rajput. Just think I could be the one pregnant by now - Yuck, what a terrible thought. I am so glad that I'm here instead. I must send her a card and congratulate her on the birth of a baby girl. Perhaps I should send something for the baby. I'll ask mum to organize it, she will know what a baby needs. No, I better not, Mum is still furious with Pretti. I'll ask Dawn.

Gosh, it's so cold; thank goodness I don't have to go out today.

I have so much work to do, who ever said that the first year at university is easy. They have really piled on the assignments this term. But I am enjoying it, the work is so interesting and I'm meeting lots of fascinating people. The guest speaker last Monday from the Water Aid charity was inspiring. Her talk was fascinating, and the work they do is extraordinary. I would love to get involved in some way.

Maybe I could do a gap year in Africa or something. Mum and Dad would probably freak out big time if I suggested that!

Well, I can dream, but for now back to that essay.

Chapter Eighteen

"I can't believe that you have found this flat, it's great," Leena said as she walked from room to room. "How did you do it?"

"Well, I have contacts," Janie tapped the side of her nose. "Things are going to get much tougher this year. I couldn't cope with the noise and distractions of the halls and, anyway, my dad is helping with the rent. So let's enjoy it," Janie said. "So, you saw this Pretti when you were home in the summer hols?"

"Yes, it was a shock. I was in the high street and suddenly there she was, with Rajput, large as life."

"So, Pretti ran off with your fiancé, this Rajput? And they are married," Janie said, "and now with a baby girl."

"Yes, little Jamilla. I was quite grateful to Pretti really, because I didn't want to marry him anyhow. I thought he was a right idiot. Anyway, they are married. Their families were furious to begin with but they have accepted it now and Pretti has moved into his family's house." Leena paused and looked around. "This flat is so great. Right on the seafront, it's fantastic."

"And they ran away to Gretna Green? I didn't think people did that anymore."

"Yes. Apparently when they got to Scotland and then found that they had to stay for a few weeks, Rajput got a job on a local building site. I can't imagine him working on a building site; he is very … well, I can't imagine it. But they ran out of money and Pretti became pregnant so they came home. Rajput family have accepted Pretti now. I think her parents kicked up such a fuss that Mr and Mrs Gowda accepted the marriage to save putting up with a lot of hassle and bad publicity. They are a vain couple and would hate to lose face."

"Wow!"

"My friend, Dawn, told me all about it. When they first came back, nobody from the family would talk to them, but they just stood firm and made the relatives accept them – fait accompli - is that how you say it? You've got to admire them really. Anyway, they did me a huge favour, so I'm not complaining." Leena paused at the door of the kitchen. "How did you find this place? It's great."

"I just couldn't endure another year in the halls of residence. The noise and squalor of it all, this is better. I have a friend, well, friend of my father; he lives in Brighton and he let me know about this place, belongs to a friend of a friend or something. We can afford it, just, with my dad's help," Janie said. "Tell me more about Pretti and this Raj..."

"That's about it. There's not a lot more to say. I've asked Sevi to see what he can find out." Leena smiled. "He will email me if there is any news."

Leena sat down on her bed and started unpacking her books, then she looked up at Janie. "You don't talk much about your family?"

"No, I don't. Mum and Dad are separated. Dad lives with his friend just outside town," Janie replied hurriedly. "Tell me more about Pretti and Raj..."

"Rajput; it was uncomfortable at first, but then I told Pretti that she had done me a favour and we were fine, had a laugh about it. She seems like quite a different person. Pretti was always so frivolous and silly and now she's quite the wife and mother. It was all very strange ... There was a bit of scandal when we were at school; Pretti got involved with her science teacher. I don't think anything really happened but she got a bad name. You know how people gossip, and in the Asian community it is easy to get a reputation or to be thought too fast..."

"I can imagine. Well, my summer was very different. I visited Dad for a week in Brighton. I went to London and saw Mum and then I went to Greece and worked as a waitress in a café next to the beach. I met this gorgeous bloke. Oh, I was nearly tempted to stay and become barefoot and pregnant, but university and my studies called. So here I am brown and broken hearted." Janie paused. "Have you seen Alum or Pieter?"

"No, but I only got back today," Leena replied.

"I met Pieter and Eggs at the takeaway last night. They are still in the halls but looking for something better."

"He likes you, you know."

Janie looked down at Leena and raised her eyebrow inquisitively.

"Who?" Janie asked with a grin. "Look, Eggs is a nice bloke, but I don't fancy him."

"No, Pieter, of course, who do you think?" Leena replied. "Why do we call him Eggs? It seems a very strange name. I've always wanted to ask."

"His name is Benedict, Benedict Pinkerton!"

"And ..."

"Benedict, you know like in eggs benedict."

Leena looked confused.

"It's a dish with eggs and hollandaise sauce ...." Janie said. "I think."

"I see," Leena said with a shake of the head, "and what about Pieter? I think he likes you. You love him, don't you?"

"Don't be daft, he doesn't even notice me when you're around; he can hardly take his eyes off you, neither of them can." Janie stopped talking and gazed out the window. "But in time ... well, you never know."

"That's not true. Anyhow, I'm not interested. Alum only likes to wind me up, and Pieter, well; he's sweet, but not my type." Leena looked perplexed. "When I was home my father started going on again about me getting married after university, but I told him not to bother, because I am never going to get married."

"Will he listen?" Janie asked standing still with an armful of text books in her arms. "I don't suppose so," Leena exhaled, "but I shall hold them off as long as possible. I do wish they would let it go."

"What will happen after university?" Janie asked.

"When I've finished my degree and graduated, I'll get my own place." Leena stood up and walked over to the window then she turned, hands on hips and looked over at Janie and then at the pile of bags on the floor. "They can't actually force me to marry anyone, can they? After all, it's against the law in this country." Leena sighed. "I suppose we'd better get sorted out, a new term starts tomorrow and things are going to get harder this year."

"I'm looking forward to getting to grips with things after the indolence of the summer. It will be good to get down to some work."

"Indolence hey, I could do with some indolence. What with my summer job and helping mum, I've come back for a rest," Leena said as she returned to the bed and unzipped one of her bags. "Did you see that report from the International Monetary Fund in the financial Times?"

"Yes, it was very interesting. Well, hopefully we will have time for some fun as well as hard work!" Janie answered with a grin. "Dad has informed me that he's expecting some good results after all the money he's spending. But one can't study all the time. We gotta have some fun!"

"I'm all for that. You know what they say, too much work and no play, saves up the play for another day," Leena laughed. "Only don't tell my mum, she thinks I'm working myself to skin and bone; hence the food-parcel." Leena indicated the large freezer bag that had been placed in the kitchen.

"Oh goody. I love your mother's cooking. But first we have to unpack." Janie looked hard at Leena. "You seem in good spirits. I was going to suggest a takeaway but as your mum's sent provisions, yummy, yummy, shall we ask the boys over, what do you think?"

"Not tonight, Janie. I'd just like to get settled in and relax. I would just like to get the feel of the place first," Leena paused. "But it's good to be back. You help yourself to the food; Mum's been filling me with chicken curry and rice all summer."

"Fine with me," Janie said, "times enough to get together and catch up tomorrow."

Janie reached for the phone and Leena started to open one of the boxes of books. "Can I use this shelf?" she asked.

"Go ahead, there's plenty of room," Janie replied.

"Who are you calling?"

"Just my father's friend to let him know we have moved in okay."

"Right," Leena said, "I'll get started on the unpacking." Then she opened an envelope, took out her timetable for the next term and sat scrutinizing it. "Crikey," Leena exclaimed and a frown appeared on her brow.

"I think things are going to be much harder this term. You want a coffee?" Janie asked.

"Yes, I think I'll need one. I've so much work to do."

"You work too hard," Janie said. "We got to have some fun too."

"No time for fun," Leena said holding up the schedule.

"But, you just said," Janie said, "you just said that 'all work and no play' was bad for us."

"That was before I saw this timetable," Leena said looking up at her flatmate. "No time for fun." Leena grimaced. "Not until I've graduated. Maybe then I can think about fun."

Leena was already reaching for her laptop.

Janie sighed and went to make some coffee.

"Here we go again," she murmured, "work, work and more work."

Chapter Nineteen

"They're having a Diwali party in Sevenoaks, there'll be lots of yummy food and a fireworks display," Leena said as she put down the phone and turned to Janie. "I wish I could go. Mum says the local recreational hall is also going to have a party with a band and all sorts of games and such."

"What, like Guy Fawkes night?" Janie looked up from her laptop and reached for the cup of coffee that Leena had made for her before answering the phone.

"Well, yes and no. Diwali is perhaps the most well-known of the Hindu festivals."

"It sounds beautiful. I've seen pictures on the TV, lanterns soaring up into the sky and candles floating on rivers and lagoons."

"The word Diwali means rows of lighted lamps. Diwali is known as the festival of lights because houses, shops and public places in India are decorated with small earthenware oil lamps called *diyas*," Leena said. "It's very beautiful, but can be dangerous; my aunt's house was nearly set on fire one year by a fire lantern that blew into her bedroom."

"No way," Janie replied. "Have you been to India? I'd love to go. Maybe I will when I leave university. I really want to travel for a while before I settle down to a job."

"I went there when I was a child. I was about eight or nine. We stayed with Aunty Lakshmi and it was quite magical. We visited the Red Fort and the Taj Majal, which is so breath taking and romantic." Leena sighed. "Mum has been saying recently that we should all go and visit when I finish university. But I don't want to go with the family because I would probably come back married to some cousin or other." Leena shrugged. "But I'd love to go again. I've always wanted to visit Kashmir and to go down to the south to Kerala and to Goa."

"Your aunt's name is Lakshmi; isn't that an India goddess?"

"Yes. For many Indians the festival honours Lakshmi, the goddess of wealth. People start the new business year at Diwali, and some Hindus will say prayers to the goddess for a successful year." Leena looked up at Janie. "Are you really interested in all this?"

"Yes. I think it's fascinating, please tell me more."

"Okay. Lamps are lit to help Lakshmi, the goddess of wealth, find her way into people's homes." Leena smiled. "We should try it. I could do with a wealth injection."

"Me too," Janie replied. "What day is it this year?"

"I think it's in the beginning of November but I'll check with Mum."

"What do we have to do?"

"Spring-clean the home, wear new clothes, exchange gifts, sweets and dried fruits, and prepare a festive meal for family and friends."

"A bit like Christmas," Janie interrupted.

"Yes, I suppose it is, but many of these religious festivals are similar. We also decorate buildings with fancy lights and, like Guy Fawkes Night, there are huge firework displays."

"It sounds great, let's do it; it will coincide with bonfire night but we can add our own special touches. What do you say, Leena? It'll be fun. We can invite the boys and some of the guys from university."

"Okay, why not," Leena said, "but it will need a bit of preparation."

"We need a break; we've been working so hard," Janie chirped. "I'll do the organizing."

"Too right," Leena added with a smile. "There's a firework display on the front in Brighton, near that big wheel thingy; we could go to that and then have our own party here afterwards. What do you think?"

"I think it'll be great."

"Good, that's settled." Leena smiled. "But, now I must get on with this essay about Bhopal that's due on Tuesday."

"Okay. I'll start getting a few things together; do you think your Mum would let us have some samosas or something? Maybe those super fish ball things she makes"

"I expect so. I'll ask next time I phone. Now I really must get on..."

Chapter Twenty

"How are things going at college," Linda asked.

"Great," Dawn replied. "What are you doing these days?"

"I'm still working at Boots the Chemist in the high road, but only three days a week. Mum wants me to go to college or university. I am not sure what I want to do. I may do something to do with pharmacy. I was quite good at science at school," Linda said. "But it seems a bit boring. I just don't know. Have you spoken to Leena lately? I've not spoken to her since she was home in the summer."

"Yes, I talked to her last week. She seems to be enjoying it down in Brighton; she's moved into a flat near the coast with her friend Janie. She'll be home for Christmas. I told her about Benji."

"It's nice down there. I've an aunt who lives in Hove," Linda said, but she was not really listening. "Look at that girl, she's huge, and she can only be about sixteen."

They were sitting in the Finch House Cafe in Tonbridge High Street drinking a coffee and waiting for Fay who was at an interview at the Town Hall. The coffee shop was quite full for a Thursday afternoon; Linda and Dawn had only just managed to get a table to themselves.

Linda always turned heads wherever she went with her blonde, English rose looks and bright blue eyes. She could be very shallow and judgemental despite being fairly intelligent, she not being blessed with much discretion. The young girl that Linda had remarked on as being fat turned out to be very pregnant. Linda grimaced and raised her eyebrows as the poor girl made her way through the tables to find a seat, her bulk almost dislodging someone's shopping trolley.

"How do you think Fay's doing at her interview?" Linda asked returning her attention to Dawn. "She should be okay; she was always good on the computer and typing, much better than me.

"What's the job?" Dawn asked.

"I think it's in the records office or something. I can't really remember."

"I know we have to learn how to use computers and such, but I still prefer to actually do things with my hands."

"That's so pretty, where did you get it?" Linda asked.

Dawn looked down at her hands; she had a henna tattoo on her wrist that looked like a vine leaf.

"At college, they wanted volunteers for the henna art class," Dawn said.

"How is it going?"

"Great, I'm learning so much about fabrics and cutting …. This term we are making clothes for puppets. They are going to be in a show at Christmas; do you want to come?"

"Yes. Why not? That reminds me. Can you make me a skirt? My gran has given me this piece of silk and I think it would make a lovely long skirt, but I have no idea how to go about it."

"Yes, I can probably do that; what colour material is it?" Dawn asked.

"It's a lovely deep blue with purple tones when it moves, it's really beautiful."

"Is there enough for a long skirt? Do you want it straight or flowing?"

"I would like it tight at the top and flowing at the bottom. Can you do that?"

"I'll have to see the material; why don't you bring it around one day this week and I'll have a look."

"That would be great, Dawn. How about Saturday morning? I have a picture that I saw in a magazine. I'll bring that along. You can keep any of the material that's left *coz* there's several meters of fabric and I won't use it. And let me know the cost of anything you need."

"Yes, that would be fine. I'm helping Benji in the afternoon," Dawn said with a grin.

"Do your parents know you're seeing him?" Linda asked.

"No, not yet," Dawn replied, "but my brother Jim knows."

Dawn had been secretly seeing Benji for some time, keeping it a secret from her parents.

"He's a great guy, Benji, but he's older than you; is that a problem?" Linda asked.

"No. I don't even think about it. We have so much in common and he encourages me to go to college, get some experience and to continue with my dressmaking and design course," Dawn said. "He's very supportive."

"His family are rich," Linda said. "Does he have any brothers or sisters?"

"So I believe," Dawn replied. "I want to tell Dad. And I will tell him soon. It's Mum that could be a problem." Dawn grinned. "Sorry. No brothers or sisters."

"Shame. I can imagine she's formidable your mum. She scares me," Linda said.

"By the way, I saw your brother, Alistair, yesterday."

"Did you? He comes to see Mum sometimes but he doesn't really bother with me or Jim and Dad avoids him," Dawn shrugged. "They fell out."

"What happened between them?" Linda asked.

"I'm not sure. Dad and Alistair never really got on, and then there was a huge row. Mum keeps in touch with Alistair, and it causes tension with Dad."

"It must be difficult," Linda said. "I heard that Alistair was into some heavy stuff, drugs and whatnot. He has a very bad reputation with the girls; my friend, Amanda, went out with him a few times. She said that he turned very nasty when she refused to sleep with him and all but raped her, if it had not been for her brother turning up." Linda shuddered.

"I heard about that; it was at a party in Ashford, I think," Dawn said quietly. "My brother's a bully and I've never trusted him … he used to drink and get into trouble, even when he was very young."

"He never touched you, did he, Dawn?" Linda asked.

"No. Dad would've killed him if he had tried anything like that with me."

"I like your dad; he's always friendly when I phone, whereas your mum is quite rude."

"Yes. Mum is very terse at times and she does badger dad; she's been better lately."

"Why's that?" Linda asked.

"Well, Dad's got a job, and that's made things a bit easier financially, taken the pressure off so to speak."

"I see, look there's Fay," Linda said waving at their friend.

Fay walked into the Finch House Café, she had a big grin on her face; she spotted her friends and waved as she made her way towards them.

"I think celebrations are on the cards," Dawn said as the two girls greeted their friend. "You look happy?"

Dawn was relieved to change the subject; she did not like talking about her brother.

"You got it." Linda asked. "You got the job?"

"Yes, I start on the 1st November."

"Yippy, let's celebrate," Linda said, "blueberry muffins?"

"My treat," Fay said running her hand through her dark brown, spiky hair, "more coffee?"

"Yes please," Linda and Dawn responded in unison.

As Fay went up to the counter to order three coffees and three blueberry muffins Linda turned to Dawn and whispered. "You have to tell your family about Benji, you know this town, they are bound to find out from someone. It would be much better if you told them yourself."

"Yes, I suppose you're right. I'll do it this weekend."

Dawn turned to Fay who had just returned with a tray loaded with coffees and muffins. "Congratulations Fay. I am glad it has worked out for you."

"Let's all go out and celebrate on Saturday night. I have met this scrummy new bloke and I want you all to meet him and Dawn can bring Benji," Linda said.

"Are you and Benji official now?" Fay asked.

"Yes, I guess we are. I am going to tell Mum and Dad about him at the weekend. We want to be together. His parents already know about me and they have been great."

"I'll drink to that," said Linda and she raised her cup of coffee in salute. "Time for celebrations all round."

"You got it," Fay said also raising her cup of coffee, "to new beginnings."

Chapter Twenty-One

"You do what?" Mrs Price said. "You must be joking."

"I have been seeing Benji Khan for several months now and we want to get engaged," Dawn said. "He's coming round tomorrow to meet you and dad…"

"I don't think so, he's an Indian. I'm not prejudiced but … I like the Purri family next door, but marry one of them, Dawn …"

"He was born in Hackney, mum," Dawn said. "He's more English than we are."

"How can he be more English than us, don't be ridiculous girl. I was born in Ireland and your dad's a London man."

"Dad was born in Wales and came to London. You were born in Ireland and came to London. Benji was born in London..."

"Don't be pedantic with me, we are white…" Mrs Price was bristling with indignation. "You can't compare…"

"And Benji's mother and father were born in England, that makes him more English than we are." Dawn looked stubbornly at her mother.

"He's not …" Mrs Price was momentarily stumped. "What will people think?"

"That he's a wonderful man … and that I love him."

"I see," Mrs Price said, running out of arguments. "He's older than you."

"He's twenty-seven, so what. He has a good job, he makes good money. His family are quite rich, they have three shops as well as the market stall, a warehouse and they import goods from India and China. His dad says that I can help in the company when I finish college and even design some clothes if I want to and we can get them made up in India."

"Humph," Mrs Price said and turned away towards the kitchen. "We'll see. Have you told your dad?"

"Not yet," Dawn said. "Jim knows and Pretti and Leena. I told her when she came home in the summer."

"Oh, and that Pretti's a fine example running away like that, getting married against her family's wishes and now she's pregnant again."

"Pretti is very happy and she's getting on well with her in-laws, they were a bit anti at first but things have settled down now."

"She's a little strumpet, stealing Leena's fiancé like that."

"Leena didn't want to marry Rajput anyway; Pretti did her a favour."

"Humph," Mrs Price grumbled. "This is different, Dawn; you don't have to marry anybody just because… Oh my god, you're not pregnant are you?"

"No Mum. I'm not pregnant, nor do I expect to be for a few years yet. I want to make something of myself, progress in my career. Mum, don't you want me to be happy?"

Mrs Price turned around and looked at her daughter; a mixture of emotions crossed her face. She'd been making a shopping list but her daughter's extraordinary news had thrown her, and now she couldn't think what she wanted to buy.

"Of course I want you to be happy, Dawn," Mrs Price said, "but life's not easy for mixed race couples. You know that."

"Things are changing, Mum. There are lots of multi-racial couples now and nobody thinks anything of it anymore."

"He's older than you," she repeated in exasperation. "What will Alistair say?"

"He won't care," Dawn said. "And it's nothing to do with him anyway."

"I don't know, are you sure about this?"

"Yes mum, I am."

"Humph," Mrs Price snorted again. "I'll talk to your father; now help me with these vegetables or we'll never get dinner ready in time. Your father will be in from work soon. I do miss him helping out around the house. But at least he has a job, that's something, hey girl?"

"Yes, mum," Dawn said reaching for some potatoes from the vegetable rack by the back door. "What are we having?"

"I've a chicken in the oven, so wash some new potatoes; leave the skins on and there are also some green beans and cauliflower. I'm making an upside down cake for dessert, with peaches, you like that, don't you?"

"Yes, mum."

"You'll have to learn how to cook curry, if you marry this Benji."

"Actually he prefers pizza."

"Humph," her mum grunted.

Chapter Twenty-Two

The Diwali party was a great success, nearly twenty people came back to Leena and Janie's little flat. They had all watched the fireworks on the seafront. It had been bitterly cold but the sky was clear and perfect for the firework display. Then they set off half a dozen brilliantly coloured lanterns from the beach and watched them sail out to sea and then everybody piled back to Janie and Leena's flat for drinks and food.

"What a night," Pieter said. "Let's have some more of that pumpkin soup. It's delicious."

"Here you go," Janie responded, ladling a huge dollop of soup into his bowl. "It's an old recipe that my mum taught me."

"It's real good," Pieter replied and then he was absorbed in spooning the steaming liquid into his mouth as fast as he could.

"You would think that he was starving to death," Alum remarked to Leena who was passing around hot jacket potatoes. "Hey, I'll have one of them," he quipped.

"Do you want cheese?" Leena asked taking a large bowl of grated cheese off the table and handing it towards Alum. She had a big grin on her face as Alum spooned a huge pile of cheese on top of his potato. "You're not hungry yourself then?" she asked.

"Well, it was bloody cold on the seafront. This was a brilliant idea from you girls. The place looks fantastic. You must have spent ages doing it up."

"It was mostly Janie, she really embraced the Diwali theme; we even have little gifts for everybody."

"The fireworks were incredible and set against the sea and the Brighton Wheel; they looked amazing." They both looked over at Janie; she was still gazing at Pieter. When she noticed Leena and Alum watching her, she quickly turned away and offered the soup to Eggs.

"Thanks Janie." Eggs accepted a bowl of soup. "What's all this Diwali stuff all about then?" he asked.

"Well, it's the Hindu festival of lights," Janie said, "which is why we are celebrating it tonight after the fireworks. Didn't you think the lanterns looked great floating off over the sea?"

"Yes. I hope none of them get blown back to land, could start a fire. But what does it all mean? I have heard of Diwali, of course, but I don't really understand what it all signifies."

"I was not too sure myself. Leena told me a bit, but I looked on the internet and it's really interesting. The festival celebrates the victory of good over evil, light over darkness and knowledge over ignorance. Although the actual legends that go with the festival vary in different parts of India. Many Hindus will leave the windows and doors of their houses open so that Lakshmi can come in. Rangoli are drawn on the floors - rangoli are patterns and the most popular subject is the lotus flower."

"That sounds amazing. I would love to go to India," Eggs said. "What are these rangoli?"

"So would I. I want to go when I finish university. " Janie paused. "I'm not quite sure; let's ask Leena. Leena," Janie called to her friend. "What exactly are rangolis?"

"Well, a rangoli is one of the arts of India," Leena said as she walked over to Janie and Eggs. "It's a traditional way of decorating courtyards and walls in Indian houses, places of worship and sometimes eating places as well. The powders are white stone, lime, rice flour and other cheap pastes that are used to draw intricate designs and patterns." Leena raised her eyebrows and continued. "I saw some beautiful ones when I went to India when I was little; after the festival they are all just washed away."

"What part of India is your aunty from?" Janie asked.

"She was from Rajasthan, but she has now moved to Gujarat. In Gujarat, the festival honours Lakshmi, the goddess of wealth," Leena replied. "In northern India and elsewhere, Diwali celebrates Rama's return from fourteen years of exile to Ajodhya after the defeat of Ravana and his subsequent coronation as king."

"I see," Eggs said. "It's all a bit confusing but very interesting."

"I find it confusing and I'm a Hindu. There are so many stories surrounding all the gods and goddesses."

"And your aunt is called Lakshmi? Is she lucky?" Eggs asked.

"Some would say she's lucky, some not. There's an Indian curse, 'May you have fourteen daughters and may they all marry well.' My aunt and uncle had ten daughters."

"I see," Eggs said looking confused again. "But…"

Leena laughed. "In India the bride's family often have to pay a dowry and all the expenses for their daughter's weddings. Having many daughters can bankrupt a family, leaving them with huge debts that can take years to repay."

"I get it," Eggs answered, "that's clever; wishing someone many daughters is cursing them to bankruptcy, fiendish."

"Yes, you got it, but Lakshmi and her husband have been fortunate, nearly all her daughters have married well, and to wealthy families. So they have reaped much back in business ties to these families and are doing very well for themselves." Leena paused. "I did want to go and visit my aunty next year. But I'm afraid that they'll try to marry me off to someone while I'm there."

"Would they do that?"

"They would have a good try," Leena laughed. "I don't intend to take the risk."

"Take Janie with you as protection," Eggs chuckled.

"Hey," Janie said, "they may try to marry me off as well."

"Who would have you," Eggs joked, "you're far too skinny."

"True," Janie said but she gave Eggs a good poke in the ribs. "I don't want to marry anyway," she said. But her eyes betrayed her as they glanced off across to a corner of the room to where Pieter was talking to a very pretty blonde girl. They seemed very deep in an intimate discussion and when Pieter intimately touched the girl's hand Janie looked away, sadness and resignation in her eyes.

Chapter Twenty-Three

The weather was icy and threatening to snow. Leena was glad to be home for Christmas and catch up with her friends, until she was again confronted by her parents' scheming.

"I think we should go to India after your graduation; we can visit aunty Lakshmi and then do some shopping and maybe go and see some sights. What do you think, Leena?" Rani asked.
"What, the whole family? Can we afford it? I don't have any money and I'd rather get straight into a job and get myself straight."

Leena was not sure about going to India with the family; she was suspicious of their motives, she felt sure that they were up to something. Aunty Lakshmi would probably have some suitors lined up for her. She didn't want to come back married to some local clodhopper or, worse still, trapped in India away from her friends and family.

"It would be just you and me; maybe your dad and Sevi could come over later when..."
"I don't think so, mum," Leena said cautiously. "I want to get a job and get settled."
"Leena, it would be such fun, just you and me, we could..."
"I can't afford it and I don't have the time right now."
"Your dad will pay for us to go, and you can find a job when you return. A few months wouldn't make much difference."
"A few months, you must be joking," Leena spluttered, now more sure than ever that her family were up to something. "No mum, maybe after a year or so when I've got myself settled. We could go on a visit then."
"But, Leena, surely it would be better to go on a lovely long holiday first and then come back and get settled into a good job. Then you could find a respectable place to live and maybe a house.

Dad and I would love to help you with a deposit for somewhere, and if you had two wages coming in it would…"

"Two wages, Mum, how am I going to have two wages?"

"When you get married, your husband…" Rani abruptly stopped talking; she knew she'd said too much, "I mean, when you get married, you will get married some time…"

"I see!" Leena said standing and putting her hands on her hips. "I will not be going to India with you and I'll not be getting married any time soon. I plan to get a good job and I plan to leave home and get a place of my own."

"Leena, you can't leave home, live on your own, what would people think?" Rani said. "You'll do as you are bid, your dad and I…"

"I will not!" Leena said and she marched out of the room leaving Rani sitting on the sofa, her mouth open, stunned and defeated.

"Well, that went well," Rani muttered to herself, "stubborn girl."

Later that day Leena went out to meet Dawn and Benji at the cafe. Dawn had told her parents that she was going to marry Benji and they were planning a small local wedding in the autumn.

"Congratulations," Leena said. "How did your parents take the news?"

"Mum was a bit anti, but we're wearing her down," Dawn said smiling at Leena. Dad was shocked but is being very supportive and Jim thinks it's great, he really likes Benji."

"My mother and father are very happy; they love Dawn like a daughter and will welcome her into the family." Benji grinned at Leena. "How could they not love her, my special, talented, beautiful girl; she will be a real asset to the family and the business."

"At this Dawn promptly blushed and took Benji's hand, he then leaned over and kissed her on the check. "It's true," he said then turning to Leena he asked, "Have you seen Pretti and Raj?"

"Not since last summer," Leena replied.

"You would hardly recognize her now," Benji said. "Did you know that she's pregnant again?"

"No. When's she due?"

"In the New Year, I'm not sure when."

"Crikey," Leena said. "Who would have thought?"

"I see her quite often, they've moved into a little house near the station and they seem very happy," Dawn said. "At least they got out of the Gowda family home."

"Yes, I can't imagine Pretti coping well living with her mother-in-law in the same house. I would hate that." Leena paused. "Well, I'm very pleased for them. She did me a huge favour. I never wanted to marry Rajput Patel. I'm really glad Pretti is finding happiness with him."

"I still can't believe that they ran away together, and now they will have two children." Benji grinned. "She sure has changed in the last three years."

"What about you. Leena, have you met anybody at university?" Dawn asked.

"No, not really," Leena replied hesitantly.

"Not really, that means that there is someone! Come on tell us all about him."

"No, there's nobody. I have made some good friends and there is Alum … and Pieter and Eggs, but no romance, we're all just good friends. I'm much too busy working hard."

"Alum, who's this Alum, is he Indian?" Dawn asked. "Come on, it can't all be hard work."

Leena looked at Benji for support, but he just shrugged.

"You got her started," he said, but at that moment the door opened.

"Goody, here's Linda and Fay," Dawn said. "I told them you were home for Christmas."

"Great," Leena said with a sigh; she was very glad to change the subject.

Leena's diary (31st January)

It was great to see my friends over Christmas. So much is happening. Fay seems to like her new job, Linda thinking of going to college. And Dawn, well she's engaged to Benji.

I would have loved to have been a fly on the wall when she told her mum that news! Mrs Price is not an easy woman, although I like her father a lot. But Benji, well he's a great guy. I think they will be very happy together.

Pretti and Rajput having another baby! Good heavens! They seem to be settling down to be the perfect couple. According to Benji, Mr and Mrs Cowden were singing Pretti's praises at the community centre a few weeks ago.

It was no surprise to hear that Dawn's brother, Alistair, has gotten into trouble. I always thought he was a bad lot. Too creepy for words! Involved in importing drugs and girls for the sex trade by all accounts! I hope they lock him up and throw away the key, the evil bastard.

This next term is going to be hard. I have so much work to do. I'd really like to get a First, but they keep piling on the assignments and things are getting more and more difficult. Even Janie and the boys are working harder this year. Janie, Pieter and Alum are working on some big population control project that sounds amazing. I'm sure that Alum will do well because he has an incredible mind. He can be very annoying at times but I do like him, even though he teases me all the time. I think he wants to get into the legal and corporation side of conservation. Probably end up working at the IMF or The World Bank or something.

I would love to do a year out on an environmental project after university. I'll contact that guy from Friends of the Earth and see if I can get involved in something. The parents will not like it but hey. . . It would be another chance to get away from them and the never ending, 'when you get married' topic. Thank goodness that Sevi had warned me that they were going to try to get me out to India next year. I must get out of that! I can't believe that Sevi is sixteen this year. He's so grown up now. They will be trying to marry him off next. My little brother so grown up, it's hard to believe.

Oh well back to the grindstone…

Chapter Twenty-Four

It is a stormy, grey day in January and Brighton's seafront is fairly empty except for the seagulls, and their raucous cries greet Lion Purri as he turns on to the promenade. He has driven down from Tonbridge to see Leena and bring some food that Rani has prepared.

"Shit, what's happening?" he says to himself.

His old Rover has started to break down. The car is making an alarmingly loud clanking noise. Lion pulls over to the pavement and gets out of the car, a confused expression on his face. He walks around to the back and bends and looks underneath. There is a dark drag mark on the road behind the car. Lion runs his hands through his wind ruffled and unruly hair.

"How far to Leena's place?" he asks himself, looking off down the road. "Rani will be mad if this food goes off."

Lion stands there helpless, hands on hips, looking around but not having any idea what to do.

On the other side of the road Alum is walking along carrying some books and toting a rucksack on his back.

"You having some trouble there, Sir?" Alum asks.

He crosses the road and goes over to the car.

"Yes, the damn thing was clunking away so much I had to stop. I'm useless with cars but I think it's something to do with the exhaust," Lion says in frustration.

"Let me have a look," Alum responds.

Alum puts down his rucksack and books on the kerb and bends to have a look under the back of Lion's old Rover.

"Can you see what's wrong? It was making a terrible noise. I'm on my way to see my daughter."

"I'm not surprised that it's making a noise; your exhaust is almost ripped off and dragging along the ground. It must have been sparking off against the road. It could have been very dangerous."

"What can I do?" Lion asks. "I've never had any trouble with it before?"

"She's a beautiful old car; Rovers are reliable as a rule," Alum says looking at Lion. "You come far?"

"Yes, from Tonbridge in Kent," Lion replies. "I've had her for so many years now. She's like an old friend to me. My wife keeps saying we should get a new car but I…"

"How far is your daughter?" Alum cuts in.

"About a mile down the road," Lion says. "It's getting very cold. I think it might snow later."

Alum nods his head and looks up at the sky. "You may be right."

"It's been a hard winter. I hope the summer is better."

"Yes," Alum replies, "me too."

Lion notices the books and backpack.

"Are you a student?" Lion asks. "Here at Brighton?"

"Yes," Alum replies.

"So is my daughter, she's at the university in her third year…"

"So am I. Do you have any string or rope in the car?" Alum asks interrupting again.

"Some string? I don't know. I may have some old rope that I used when I had to give my neighbour a tow last year."

Lion opens the boot of the car and rummages around until he finds a length of rope about two meters long.

"Will this do?" he asks, holding up the piece of old rope.

"Yes, that will do fine but only as a temporary measure, mind."

Alum gets down on the road and manages to tie up the exhaust pipe so that it's not hanging down on the tarmac. In the process he gets his jeans very dirty from the nearby gutter.

"There you are, Sir, that will get you to your daughter, but then you must call a garage and get it fixed properly. It's not safe to drive any long distances."

"Thank you very much," Lion says. "I don't know what I would have done without you. Oh dear, look at your trousers they have got so dirty. Please let me give you something for your trouble."

Lion gets some money out of his pocket and offers it to Alum, but Alum shakes his head and puts his palm up in negative gesture.

"No. I can't take anything; it was a pleasure to help."

"But, your trousers, they are filthy," Mr Purri says looking down at Alum's soiled knees. "Let me give you something to get them cleaned."

"No, don't trouble yourself, they will wash. Now you call a garage as soon as you can. I can't say how long that rope will hold your exhaust pipe in place."

Alum picks up his backpack and books and starts to walk away down the street.

"At least tell me your name," Lions calls after him.

Alum stops and turns with a big smile.

"It's Alum, sir, Alum Contem. Bye now. Enjoy your visit with your daughter and get that fixed properly before driving home."

Alum continues to walk off down the street and Lion stands and watches him as he goes, then Alum turns to wave his hand.

"Bye Sir," he says. "Have a good visit."

Lion watches as Alum strides off down the seafront.

"Now why can't my Leena meet a nice boy like that?" Lion says quietly to himself then he gets back into his car and drives slowly away down the road.

Chapter Twenty-Five

It had been a hard autumn term and apart from the Diwali party there had been little time for socializing in November and December. Christmas had come and gone and abruptly the girls are looking forward to their last two terms at university.

Janie, Alum and Pieter are sitting on the living room floor and studying for their project. Leena is sitting reading on her bed.
"Can I get anyone more coffee?" Leena asks, coming into the front room.
"Thanks," Janie and Alum reply. Pieter looks up at Leena, a wistful expression on his face.
"Okay. But first I'm going to take these food containers to the bin outside. And then I'm going to post a letter." Leena gathers up the remains of their takeaway meal.
"Thanks Leena," Janie says. "I think we need some mental stimulation."
"I'll put the kettle on," Leena says, going into the kitchen. "I need some air; it smells too much like home in here."
She empties the bin and puts the empty food boxes into the black sack and takes it outside. When she returns, Leena makes the coffee and give them all a mug and goes and sits back down on her bed.
"It looks like snow," she says, "and it's bloody cold."

Alum has gulped down his coffee but Pieter, who seems preoccupied, has put his down absentmindedly on the table next to him. He has also not touched much of the Indian takeaway meal, unusual for him.

"We could divide the subject into three parts and we could each present one part?" Janie says. "What do you think?"
"Yes, that would work. What do you think Pieter?" Alum replies, looking intently at Pieter who was not really listening. He is seated

on the floor near the door and trying to catch sight of Leena in her bedroom.

"What?" Pieter says suddenly jerking his head back to focus on Alum.

"Three parts, one each?" Alum suggests; a glint of humour in his eyes.

"What are you doing? Do you want to work on this project or not?" Janie asks.

"Yes. Well, three parts, that makes sense. We could do an introduction then relate our sections and open it up to questions," Pieter says, dragging his mind back to the question of their project. But even then he looks back around at where Leena is sitting in the other room. "I'm paying attention, it's just that…"

"I have some good slides and charts we could use on the overhead via my laptop. What about a hand-out and some statistics?" Janie asks, reaching into her briefcase and bringing out a file of papers which she puts on the small table in front of Alum.

"Great, I'll cover the economic issues of overpopulation. Janie the moral issues and Pieter can dress up as a clown."

Alum looks fixedly at Pieter who is still not paying attention. In fact, he is still looking towards the bedroom.

"Sounds good," Pieter says distractedly.

Alum and Janie look at each other and start to laugh and end up rolling around on the floor in hysterics. Pieter looks back at them, only just realizing what had been said.

"Very funny, but I am willing to try anything to improve my grades this year!" he says, and then he starts to laugh. "I suppose I have been a bit distracted."

At that moment Leena comes out of her room, carrying her overcoat, and looks at them as if they are all mad. But she smiles as they sprawl on the floor giggling.

"What are you lot up to?" Leena asks, as she looks down at the three hysterical figures as they roll about consumed in uncontrollable mirth.

"We are working out our population and birth control presentation," Janie answers, dissolving into giggles once again.

"I see," Leena says. "And I thought it was a serious subject. Well you know what the famous man said, if you can keep your head when all around are losing theirs, you obviously are not seeing the entire problem. Or something like that!"

"Thanks Leena, that's very helpful," Alum says.

"That's my role, helpful to a T." Leena laughs. "Anyway, I am going to post a letter and I might go for a walk along the seafront."

"But, it must be zero degrees out there," Janie says. "Take your umbrella; it looks as if we are going to have a downpour. I'd not noticed how dark it's got."

"Yes, but there's going to be a glorious sunset," Leena answers as she picks up her bag and heads for the door.

"We finished now?" Pieter says jumping up from the floor.

"Well, not really. We need to ..." Alum starts to say.

"I'll come with you, Leena. I need to go anyway," Pieter interrupts Alum and grabs up his jacket.

"But Pieter, wait..." Alum shouts, "What the hell?"

"What about your coffee?" Janie yells, "Pieter?"

Pieter ignores them and as he pulls on his jacket he knocks Janie's file to the floor. Oblivious, he follows Leena out of the flat and then they hear the front door bang.

Alum and Janie look at each other in amazement.

"Pieter, you have forgotten your books," Janie yells after him, but he has disappeared. "Pieter off his coffee and food, not a good sign," Janie murmurs to herself.

"He's gone, he didn't seem to be here anyway, or his mind wasn't in any case." Alum says. "What's wrong with him?" Alum looks towards the front door.

"I have a fair idea," Janie answers sadly, starting to gather up her papers.

Janie turns away so that Alum can't see the tears that have sprung to her eyes.

"Want a cup of tea?" she asks.

"I'd prefer another coffee?" he asks turning back to Janie and handing her his empty mug.

Janie goes into the kitchen to make more coffee, as she stands in front of the kettle she gives herself a little shake and wipes a tear from her cheek.

"I'm a fool," she tells herself, "a very silly, bloody fool."

She takes down the biscuit barrel from the cupboard and puts a selection on a plate and then carries it back into the sitting room. She puts the mug of coffee down in front of Alum.

"Want a biscuit? So what was that all about?" Janie asks with a smile. "He's acting a bit crazier than usual."

"Pieter's got a thing for Leena," Alum replies reaching for the coffee. "He told me he was going to make a play for her, if I didn't mind."

"You're kidding me. I always thought it was you who would …" Janie says, but then she turns her head away so he can't see her face. "Well, you both may need that clown suit after all."

"Me?" Alum says, "why me?" Alum looks at Janie quizzically and then he stretches and shrugs his shoulders. "Gosh, my neck is stiff."

"You like her, don't you?" Janie asks.

"Yes, course I do. She's a great girl, our little 'greenie' but…" Alum pauses and looks directly at Janie. "You don't think she would be interested in him. Do you?"

"No, Leena's set against men; she wants to have a career. And I don't think she would be interested in Pieter even if..." Janie looks sadly at Alum. "Poor Pieter, you do know that if she was interested in anyone, it would not be Pieter, it would be you. Don't you?"

"Don't be absurd, she can't stand me, we argue all the time." Alum turns and looks at Janie with a concerned face. "He'll realize that you're the girl for him eventually, Janie."

"What?" Janie says looking shocked. "He's a twit."

"You can't fool me, Janie," he says. "I know you love the bastard. Even if he's too thick to notice what a gorgeous girl you are. What an idiot."

"Steady there," Janie says then she smiles at Alum. "You can fool yourself though, can't you?"

"I don't know what you mean," he says looking confused.

"Oh. You will, you will," she answers with a shrug. "Maybe we all need clown suits."

They sat drinking their coffee and both their faces are thoughtful as they relax, silently thinking their own private thoughts. Alum seems confused but he also looks as if he had just realized something very important. He then glances towards the door again and shrugs and shakes his head.

"No, you're crazy, girl. Obviously working too hard; what we need is a bit more fun," Alum says.

"What's fun? With the amount of work I have to do this term," Janie says. "We will see Alum." Janie turns away and a sad, secret smile comes to her face. "We will see."

Chapter Twenty-Six

On the promenade outside dusk was falling fast. The sky was still a bright electric blue, but there were low dark grey clouds on the horizon. With the diminishing light the sunset was starting to deepen, the rose pink hued clouds turning darker into shades of salmon and crimson set against a pale yellow tinted sky. The darker clouds in the east looked heavy with foreboding.

Pieter ran out of the flat, still fastening his jacket. He was panting and out of breath as he tried to follow to Leena.

"Wait, Leena, wait. I'll walk with you," Pieter said, catching his breath. "God, it's so cold."

Leena stopped and waited for him to catch up, tilting up her coat collar against the wind. She looked back at him then turned her face up to the sky.

"Hi Pieter, I thought you lot were all going to be planning your presentation this evening," she said. "I think it's going to snow."

"Well. We have sorted it out; we are going to do a piece each. I am going to do..."

"Oh," Leena said, looking at Pieter questioningly.

"Well, I am ..." Pieter stopped talking, suddenly realizing that he did not know what part he was supposed to be preparing. "Well, I'll see them tomorrow ... and find out what I'm doing."

"I see!" Leena said. Then she laughed and shook her head. "Janie will have it all planned out; she's very organized this term."

"No bother. I'll speak to Alum later anyway and he'll let me know what's happening."

They walked along together in silence until they reached the post-box and Leena posted her letter. Then Leena crossed over to the railing and looked out over the sea. The sunset was now quite glorious, a wash of vibrant colour. Pieter followed her and stood close beside her. They stood gazing up into the darkening winter sky. The sea looked very grey and dark except where there were the last golden ripples of the setting sun on the horizon and the tips of the rollers. Behind them the sky was threatening an imminent downpour, the clouds heavy with moisture and the wind bitterly cold.

"Leena," Pieter said softly.

"Yes, Pieter," Leena replied turning to face him and leaning her arms on the railing.

"Do you like me?" he asked her, his voice low and rasping in the night air.

"Course I do" she said. "Why do you ask?"

Pieter suddenly leaned over and kissed her on the lips. Leena jerked away, taken by surprise. Pieter moved towards her again and tried to put his arm around her shoulders. "What are you doing?" Leena said, taking a step backwards.

"But - you said you liked me."

"I do like you, Pieter, but not like that."

"It's Alum, isn't it?

"What are you talking about?" Leena said looking confused. "Have you lost your mind?"

"You like Alum, don't you?" Pieter said, his face crumbling.

"Well, of course I like Alum," Leena said. "But not as a boyfriend. We ... we are just friends that's all." Leena sighed. "I don't have time for boyfriends."

"Of course you don't. You are far too busy," he said bitterly.

"Pieter, I have fought very hard to get to university. I can't waste time on boys. I have to work hard and get my degree so I can have my independence. And then maybe after ..."

"Your precious independence, is that all you can think about? What about having some fun? Oh, Leena, you're so beautiful." Pieter went to move towards her again, but she quickly moved away and put out her hand up to stop him coming closer.

"No, Pieter," Leena said. "I don't have time for this."

"I see," he said. "I'll go then."

Pieter stormed off leaving Leena standing alone. She shook her head and pulled up the collar of her coat once more. The sunset was still beautiful, but as she stood, hands deep in her pockets, she felt the first wet spots on her face as it gently started to snow. Leena stood and watched the sunset. The falling white snowflakes looked like golden confetti from the reflection of the fading sun, but gradually they faded to a dull grey. The snow started to fall thicker and she shivered as the promenade slowly turned white. Leena looked up at the grey sky and blinked a snowflake from her eyelashes.

"Well, I had better get back, it's getting very cold. I can't believe what just happened," she muttered. "Pieter is just… well … I just can't believe…"

By the time Leena returned to the flat, Alum had left, Janie had washed up the mugs and was sitting on her bed with her head in one of her books.

"Janie," Leena said looking around, "has Alum gone?

"Yes," Janie said, but she did not look up and continued reading her book.

"Pieter tried to kiss me," Leena said, "just now, today outside on the seafront."

Janie's head shot up and she looked hard at Leena.

"What," she said and then she muttered to herself. "Roll on the clowns." Janie stood up and faced Leena. "What happened?"

"When I went to post my letter, he followed me. We were standing by the seafront and he kissed me. He tried to kiss me."

They stood gazing at each other in silence for a few seconds and then Janie sat down again.

"And … I thought he liked you," Leena said.

"He does, he does. He just doesn't know it yet."

"I don't understand," Leena said, taking off her coat. She sat down on the edge of the bed. "It's so cold and it's started to snow."

"Men are like that, stupid; they don't see what's in front of them," Janie said. "Pieter is like that and so is Alum."

"Alum, what's this to do with Alum?" Leena said.

"Alum loves you."

"What ... what?" Leena stuttered. "What the hell are you talking about? Alum doesn't love me."

Leena looked so shocked. She took a book from the shelf and opened it distractedly. Then she put it down on the bed and gazed at Janie as if she had two heads.

"Men are so stupid and so it appears are you," Janie said.

"I don't understand what you're saying," Leena said, glaring at her friend.

"Look," Janie said talking very slowly, looking up at Leena. "I love Pieter. Pieter does not yet know it, but he loves me. Alum loves you and you love Alum. Only neither of you knows it - yet."

"Have you gone completely mad?" Leena asked.

"Yes, and we are all wearing clown suits," Janie said as she sat down heavily and looked down again at her book. Leena stared down at Janie, with an incredulous look.

"I think you've been working too hard."

"Yes, that must be it," Janie said then she laughed and turned her face away so that Leena could not see the tears in her eyes.

Janie carried on reading and Leena looked on with a confused expression on her face.

"I am going to make some soup. It's dreadfully cold out. Do you want anything?" Leena said heading for the kitchen.

"Not hungry," Janie muttered.

Leena's diary (February 4Th)

There's snow on the ground today and it's really cold, but it looks so beautiful.

Well, I wouldn't have believed it but yesterday Pieter tried to kiss me! I was down on the seafront to post a letter to my aunty Kalpane. He followed me and well, he kissed me! I was so shocked.

Janie, Alum and Pieter had been working on their diversity project at the flat. I wanted to see the sunset and get a bit of fresh air. It was very cold and threatening to snow but the sunset was glorious. Pieter followed me and then he asked me if I liked him. I said yes - but then he kissed me. I had to explain that I liked him but not in that way. Then he asked if I loved Alum. Strange! Then he rushed off in a huff. But why did he ask me that? It's odd, but I can't be angry with him. He said that I only think about myself and getting good grades and not about anything else. Is that true? I suppose I am very motivated but I had to fight hard to get to university and it's important that I get a good degree so I can have my independence. I hope I don't come across detached and uncaring!

When I returned to the flat, Alum had gone and Janie was acting very strangely, muttering something about men being such fools; well, I know that already.

I told her about Pieter, but then she said that Alum loved me. She was also mumbling something about dressing up in clown suits. Seriously cracked!

We have all been under so much pressure this term.

But to say something like that! Alum in love with me?

Do you think that it can be true? He's always teasing me or alternatively he just treats me with indifference. I think, Janie has been working too hard. Is she in love with Pieter? And is that why she's acting so oddly? I don't know what's going on. I do care about Alum, but love ...

Well, I must close now. I have so much work to do. I will be sad when university ends. I do hope we can all keep in touch.

Could Alum really be in love with me? No, it's too ridiculous for words. Janie must be going crazy, it's all this hard work we are doing. Talking of work I must get off to my IT development class. Not my favourite subject but I can't fail this class as it will bring my scores down. The world relies on computers these days.

Must phone mum later!

Part Three

Chapter Twenty-Seven

"That's it then," Alum says as he pauses to take a sip of coffee from a polystyrene cup, "all over."

"Yes, the last exam. Thank god." Pieter stretches up his arms and then flops back onto the grass. "It's hard to imagine it, going into real life, no more university."

The sun is shining; Alum and Pieter are sitting on the grass verge. They have just had their final exams.

"What a beautiful day," Pieter says. "It's great to be alive."

It was indeed a glorious day, sunny and warm and there were several other students lounging on the grass and celebrating the end of term. Some had brought a bottle of wine or some beers and were having an impromptu party. The atmosphere was happy, relaxed and there was a sense of closure and relief in the air.

"What are you going to do after graduation?" Alum asks.

"I'm going to go back to Denmark. I may travel for a few months and then find a job," Pieter replied. "And you? Will you see Leena?"

"I expect we will keep in touch. What about you and Janie?"

"She's going to come to Denmark with me and meet the family and we'll come back for the graduation ceremony and then see where things go from there. But I mean what about you and Leena?"

"Me and Leena?" Alum looks down at Pieter, a puzzled expression on his face.

Pieter sits up. He picks up his coffee, drinks a swig of it and then looks straight at Alum.

"God, Janie is right, some men are so stupid."

"What do you mean?" Alum splutters. "Anyway you can talk, how long did it take before you realized that you loved Janie?"

"She told me, but I sort of knew anyway," Pieter says. "I mean, I was a bit silly about Leena for a time there but it's so obvious now that she was not meant for me. You do like her, don't you?"

"Janie told you?" Alum asks. He picks up his coffee and is turning the container around and around in his hands.

"Yes, she just said, 'Now look here you twit, I love you.' And I suddenly realized that I loved her too."

"Wow."

"Sometimes we need the obvious pointed out to us."

"We do?" Alum says, putting down the empty coffee container and reaching for another blueberry muffin. "These are good," he mumbles with his mouth full.

"You love Leena, you idiot. Are you going to let her get away?"

There is a pause while Alum eats his muffin, then a look of confused realization came to his face.

"But …" Alum pauses, his mouth gapping open. "Leena has made it clear to anyone who would listen that she's not interested in men, or getting married. That she wants a career. I do care about Leena, but I don't think she thinks of me that way. Our little 'greenie' has other priorities."

"That's what she has always said, true. She always said that her priority was to get through university and get her degree." Pieter looks down at his coffee.

"And now she has got her degree or as near as, seeing as she has got top marks all throughout her course," Alum says. "I expect she'll walk away with a First."

"Yes. I expect she will. And …" Pieter glances up and raises his eyebrows questioningly.

"So you think that she might be interested in me," he pauses, "now that she's finished university."

"Of course she's interested in you."

"Really?" Alum looks dumfounded as if the idea had never occurred to him.

"You are a fool! Leena loves you, for heaven's sake. Go and tell her that you love her too, before it's too late. Phone her now, before she leaves," Pieter says.

Alum looks down and picks a daisy from the grass; he sits and twiddles with it for a few seconds.

"When's she leaving?" he asks.

"Today," Pieter says. "Janie said she was going home today."

Alum reaches into his pocket for his mobile phone and starts to speed dial Leena's number.

"It's engaged. I'll go to the flat," Alum says.

"Janie told me that Leena's family is picking her up later on today."

"Thank God for that. I'll go now and then get the train from Brighton station. I'm all packed and ready."

"If you had let that girl get away, I …" Pieter says. "Well, I don't know what I would do. Just don't muck it up."

Alum gathers up his stuff and sets off towards the gate. He turns and waves at Pieter, the expression on his face aglow with realization.

"Thank you, Pieter, and goodbye. I hope things work out well for you and Janie."

"Goodbye Alum and good luck. See you at graduation."

Pieter relaxes back onto the grass and throws his arms wide laughing to himself.

"Eureka!" he shouts.

The time is just before 2.15 pm

Chapter Twenty-Eight

The bedroom of Janie and Leena's flat is in disarray, boxes of books and half-packed cases scattered on every available space, but there are also a neat pile of boxes and a large trunk sitting next to the front door. Janie is packing and Leena is sitting on the floor with a book in her lap.

"You're so organized and look at me leaving everything to the last minute," Janie said. "What's the time?"

"It 2.30," Leena replied. "When are you leaving?

"First thing in the morning," Janie said looking down at Leena. "I'm going to leave most of my stuff at my dad's friend in Brighton, and then go off to Denmark with Pieter to meet his family. Exciting, isn't it? And you?"

Leena is not really listening but gazing into the open book on her lap; she is not actually reading it and she does look up and answer Janie.

"Dad just phoned to say that they will pick me up at 5 o'clock ..." Leena says, and then she smiles up at Janie. "Can I help? With the packing, I mean."

"No, thank you, I'll do it. I've got to organize what to take and what to store," Janie answers.

"I can't believe it's all over," Leena says.

"Yes, I don't quite believe that three years could pass so quickly," Janie replies. "And how did I get all this stuff? I will never be able to carry it."

"Yes, in a few months' time we will have graduated and then ..." Leena pauses, and looks down at her book. "Well, the rest of our life is in front of us. You are still planning to go to Denmark?"

Janie looks down at Leena with a raised eyebrow and a surprised look. "Yes. I'm going to stay with Pieter and his family and then, well, we'll see. But we both want to travel before settling down to jobs and such like." Janie pauses and then turns to reach a pile of papers from a shelf and puts them into a box. Then she turns back to talk to Leena running her hands through her wild, curly red hair, "but what about you Leena?"

"Well, I'm going to have to stay with my parents at first. I want to find a good job. I have applied to that Water Aid charity and I've had a few other leads but nothing definite yet and then I want to get my own place. This will be difficult. My mother will not want me to live on my own, but I need to have my own space. We'll keep in touch, Janie. I may even come and visit you in Denmark. Have you seen Alum?"

"No, I think that he's getting the train from Brighton up to London today," Janie says. "I believe he has a good job to go to and a flat in Islington all sorted. He'll most probably get a good degree. I wouldn't be surprised if he got a First. Like you!"

"I haven't got a First yet. And I won't believe it until I see it."

"Oh, but you will, you have done better than anyone this year." Janie pauses again and looks directly at her friend. "Go and see Alum before it's too late."

"What, before what's too late?" Leena asks.

"Oh, Leena for God's sake," Janie says in exasperation. "You can't tell me that you want that boy to walk out of your life today and never see him again?"

"No. But I don't know how he feels about me."

"If one of you doesn't make a move you will never know," Janie exclaims.

"What should I do? I'll phone him."

Leena gets up and picks up her phone. Then she sits back down on the edge of the bed and looks blankly up at Janie.

"Do it," Janie commands.

Leena punches in Alum's mobile number. "It's engaged," she says clicking off the phone, "and my batteries are getting low, I'd better charge it."

"Go over to his place before he leaves."

"I can't. Can I?"

"Go. For heaven's' sake go," Janie says, "Go and see him."

Leena grabs up her bag and dashes out of the room, leaving her mobile phone behind on the bed. She nearly trips over one of her carrier bags in her haste to get out. The door slams and Janie is left standing open mouthed. "About time," she mutters. "I hope she catches him."

Janie smiles to herself and carries on with her packing.

The time is now 2.45.

Chapter Twenty-Nine

It is just after 3.00 pm when Alum collects his cases from his digs and goes next door to leave the keys with his landlady.

"Thank you for everything, Madge. I'll keep in touch. I'll certainly come and visit you again soon," Alum says. "You've been great."

"Good luck to you, Alum, you would be welcome anytime," Madge says taking the keys and dropping them into her skirt pocket. "What are your plans? I know you have a job but what first, you're going on holiday, aren't you?"

"I'm getting the train up to London today. But I am going to have a holiday before starting work. I'm going to the USA to visit my cousin and his family in Houston for two weeks."

"That sounds good. I have always wanted to go to Texas," Madge says. "Well, it's been a pleasure to have you stay. Good luck, Alum. Are you keeping in touch with Pieter and the others?"

"I sure am. I may go and visit Pieter and Janie in Denmark."

"And, what about that pretty Indian girl, Leena, was it? Will you be seeing her?"

"I hope so," Alum responded. "I do hope so."

"She's lovely and so intelligent too."

"Yes, she is. I expect she will get a First. Thanks for everything. Bye Madge. Please send on any mail."

"I will do that. No problem. You take care now." Alum hugs Madge and she kisses him on the cheek.

"I'll miss you," she says.

Alum leaves the building and heads off down the road. The time is now 3.05 pm. He hails a taxi and gets into it and disappears down the road.

As Alum vanishes in one direction Leena appears from another, on foot. She is running, out of breath and nearly blinded by tears of frustration. Leena goes into the building and knocks frantically at the door of Alum's old flat. There is no answer. Madge hears the knocking and comes out to see what the noise is all about.

"Alum, are you there? Alum," Leena shouts knocking frantically at the door.
"Can I help you, dear?" Madge asks Leena. "Are you okay?"
"I'm looking for Alum," Leena says tearfully.
"He just left, my love."
"Where has he gone?" Leena gasps.
She is still winded from her run down the seafront and her face is flushed and red.
"He has gone into Brighton to get the train to London."
"Oh no," Leena wails. Leena then turns around and dashes off leaving Madge standing there looking perplexed.
"You should catch him if you hurry, dear," she shouts. "He only left five minutes ago."

Leena rushes out into the street and runs over to the bus stop to get the bus to Brighton station. She looks at the timetable and then looks exasperated. She glances around but there is no sign of a taxi.
"I'll phone him," Leena says as she searches in her bag and then realizes that she had left her phone behind. "Oh damn and blast," she says to herself.

Chapter Thirty

Alum alights from the taxi at Brighton station with his cases. He looks very harassed as he goes to buy a ticket at the ticket office. He glances up at the station clock; it is 3.20 pm.

'I'll put the luggage in the left luggage,' he thinks, narrowly missing an elderly woman who is trying to pull her huge red suitcase into the line of people waiting for tickets.
"Sorry," he mutters, rushing off towards the back of the station.
"Careful," the woman yells after him as he dashes away.
After depositing his luggage, Alum tries Leena's mobile number but there is still no answer.
"Bloody hell," he mutters. "Where are you?"

Alum is in a panic as he leaves the station, peering around anxiously. His normal calm demeanour is shattered; it is as if he has had a sudden epiphany, how could he not have seen it before?
'I love her, bloody hell, I have been so blind,' he thinks as he rushes down the street towards Janie and Leena's flat. He sees a taxi and hails it.

Chapter Thirty-One

Leena gets off the bus and runs into Brighton station; it is 3.45 pm. She is looking around frantically and bumps into a stout lady who is trundling along with a huge red suit case.

"Sorry," Leena says, as she steadies the woman and rushes towards the ticket office.
"Look where you're going, can't you," the woman shouts, glaring at Leena. "Bloody kids today, always in such a hurry."

"What time is the next train to London?" Leena asks the man in the ticket office.
"3.55, Miss, do you want a ticket?" he replies.
"No, thank you. What platform?"
"Platform two," the man answers.
Leena runs off towards the trains, the ticket seller calls after her.
"You'll need a platform ticket, Miss."
She does not hear him as she races off to find the platform, but when she gets to the turnstiles she can't get through.
"Can I get onto the platform?"
"Not without a ticket," the guard says.
"But I need to see someone who is getting on this train."
"You still need a platform ticket, Miss," he replies.
"But … where?" Leena is now getting more and more exasperated.
"Ticket office," the man says turning away with a shrug.

Leena turns and sprints back to the ticket office; there is now a line of people. She stands on one foot and then the other until finally her turn comes and she buys a platform ticket.
The time is now 3.52 by the station clock.

"Platform ticket, please," she asks impatiently.

Leena takes her ticket and runs back to platform two, clutching her side as stitch starts to burn in her chest. She passes onto the platform as the train doors are closing. It is just 3.55 and the London train pulls away.

Leena races down the platform trying to look into the carriages, but the train leaves the platform behind and she is left standing watching as it disappears. Leena bends forward, her hands on her knees and she pants and clutches her rib cage, then she turns back towards the station entrance; tears are now running down her cheeks.

People turn and stare at her, this beautiful Asian girl, so dishevelled and anguished, who seems so lost and distraught, but Leena does not notice them in her despair.

"Are you okay?" a lady in a bright summer dress asks.
"Oh no," she cries in frustration. "I've missed him again."
"I'm sorry," the woman says looking confused.
"I'm okay, I have missed my friend," Leena sobs, "and he does not know that I love him." Then Leena dashes off before the woman can say any more. But she stands back and watches as Leena rushes up the platform.
"How sad," she says. "I hope she finds him."

Chapter Thirty-Two

A taxi pulls up outside Leena and Janie's flat and Alum gets out and rushes to the entrance. He enters the front door, charges up the stairs and rings the bell looking around anxiously. Janie answers and a look of anguish comes to her face.

It is now 4 o'clock.

"Bloody hell, Alum, what are you doing here?" she says, staring at Alum in astonishment and alarm.

"Hi Janie, is Leena here?"

"No. She has gone to find you."

"Where?" he asks her his hand raking through his hair, making it stand on end.

"Why, at your digs. What time are you…" Janie starts to say but Alum interrupts.

"But, I just left there. I am on my way home to London. When will she be back?

"I don't know; but her family are coming for her at 5 pm to take her back to Tonbridge."

"I'll wait," Alum says going and sitting down on the sofa. "Is she… okay?"

"Yes, she's okay, but she will be sorry to have missed you. Do you mind if I get on with my packing?" Janie says. "I'm afraid I'm not very organized."

Alum nods and looks down at his hands; there is a noise outside and he gets up and goes over to the window.

"You seeing Pieter?" he asks and then goes and sits on the bed again, he picks up a book and looks through it.

"Yes, we're going to Denmark to meet his family."

"That's nice," he says distractedly, putting the book down beside him, nearly covering the phone and its charger that are lying there. He sees the phone and pushes it aside so that it is nearly obscured by the pile of bed linen.

Janie continues with her packing. Time passes and Alum gets up and walks backwards and forwards across the room. Alum looks out the window again and then sits down again and then he looks at his watch anxiously. After a short while he gets up again and tries his phone again. Leena's phone starts to ring, where she has left it lying on the bed, next to him, in the flat.

"She left her phone behind," Janie says. "She was in such a panic."

"Look," he said, cutting off his phone and stuffing it into his jacket pocket. "I have to go, I have a ticket for the 4.45 train. This is hopeless. Can I leave a note for Leena?"

"Yes. Of course, I will give it to her when she gets back."

"Have you got some paper and an envelope?" Alum asks.

"Sure thing, here you are," Janie says as she passes Alum some paper and an envelope and he writes a quick note and puts in into the envelope and addresses it to L Purri.

It is now 4.30 pm.

"Bye Janie, I wish you all the best I hope it all works out well for you and Pieter."

"We'll see, take , Alum. I will give this to Leena," Janie says, indicating the note that Alum has put on the table. "See you at graduation?"

"Yes, graduation," he mutters. "You'll send the note?"

"I'll send it. Don't worry."

"Bye, Janie." Alum paused. "It's been great. Thanks for all your support."

"You too, now give us a hug and get going and don't worry," Janie says and pats the note that is lying on the table. They embrace and Janie gives Alum a quick kiss on the cheek and then Alum leaves.

Janie carries on with her packing. She takes a pile of books off a shelf and puts them onto the table. Unnoticed by Janie the note is now buried under her pile of books. Janie carries on doing her packing unaware that she has hidden the note.

Ten minutes later at 4.40, Leena re-enters the flat. She has been crying, she is red faced and she looks absolutely exhausted.

"Leena, my god what has happened? Did you see him?" Janie asks.

"No, I missed him at his digs. His landlady said he had gone to the station, so I went to the station but I missed the train. And … oh what a mess!" she sobs.

"Calm down, Leena. Calm down, he was here. You just missed him. He left a note. Wait a minute, where is it?" Janie looks around, but she can't find the note. "It was right here."

"He was here, but where has he gone?"

"He has gone to catch his train – now, where the hell is that note? Janie mutters frantically lifting piles of books.

"I must go and find him," Leena says then promptly bursts into tears. "I'll try to phone him. Now where is my phone?" Leena locates her phone which is half obscured by a pile of bed linen. She picks it up and dials Alum's number from the address book. "It's ringing. Oh shit, what now." The phone has gone completely lifeless; she has forgotten to plug it into the charger. "The battery is still dead, Oh shit, shit, shit." She sits down on the bed, head in hands and starts to cry again.

"Charge it now," Janie says, in a wild eyed frenzy. "Now, where is that bleeding note?"

"I must charge it," Leena says, not hearing her friend, standing up and looking imploringly at Janie. "I've really messed everything up, Janie, what am I going to do?"

"Charge your phone and don't worry," Janie mutters, she's standing with her arms full of books looking crazily around the room.

Leena plugs her phone into the charger, making sure that she has turned on the switch, leaving it on the bed that she had stripped earlier. She goes over to the window still crying, looks out then goes back over to the bed and sits fiddling with her hair; she picks up her handbag and starts to rummage through it as if there would be some clue in there as to where to find Alum.

"Calm down, Leena," Janie says. "You will have missed his train now. He said he was catching the 4.45, but, I'm sure it will all be okay. I promise you ..."

Leena looks up at Janie. "Where did you put the note?" she asks.

"I don't know; it was right here."

While she is saying this Janie puts down the pile of books and starts to rummage through a box of packed things looking for the note. Leena is crying again and Janie is getting more frantic by the second. The only thing Janie is achieving is to pile more and more books on top of the already buried note. "It was just here."

Then they heard a car honking from the street outside and Janie goes over to look out the window.

"Now, calm down, Leena. Your family is here," Janie says as she turns to Leena, grabbing a handful of tissues from the dressing table which she passes to the distraught girl. "Tidy yourself up, or your folks will worry."

"But, I'm not ready. Oh, Alum, I ..." Leena looks up at Janie imploringly. "What am I going to do?"

"Wipe your eyes," Janie says, again looking around frantically before glancing back at Leena. "Come here and give me a hug. I'll find it."

"But ... Oh Janie, I love him."

Leena stands and pulls a face, Janie hands her another tissue and gives her a squeeze.

"I know," Janie says. "It'll be okay. You'll see. I have your address."

Footsteps and voices are heard outside and then there's a knock on the door.

"Leena, are you there?" Rani calls.

Leena turns and goes to open the door. The Purri family enter. Lion, Rani and Sevi; they are all looking cheerful and happy.

"Hi," Leena says limply.

"Whatever's wrong, Leena?" Rani asks. Seeing Leena's face she goes over immediately and looks at her closely. "Have you been crying?"

"I'm okay, Mum, we were just saying goodbye, that's all," Leena mutters turning away.

"Yes, Mrs Purri. I'm really going to miss your Leena so very much," Janie says.

"You will still see each other, Janie, you know that you are welcome to visit us anytime," Mr Purri says.

"Why, thank you, Mr Purri. I surely will," Janie responds.

"Are you ready, Leena? I want to avoid the traffic," Mr Purri says.

"Yes Dad, all packed. You okay, Sevi?" Leena asks. "School finished?"

"Yes Leena, how about you?" Sevi grins, "a few weeks of freedom."

"I'm fine," Leena says but as she replies she turns to Janie with an enquiring look. "You will find it?"

"I'll find it." Janie looks around her as she speaks. "It was just here," she looks at the table that is now covered with her books. "I'll send it on to you. Don't worry Leena."

"What's up, Leena?" Rani asks.

"We have lost something, that's all," Leena says.

"I'll find it. Don't worry," Janis says emphatically. "I'll send it on."

Leena and Janie hug again and then the Purri family leave all laden down with the one huge case, boxes and carrier bags - leaving Leena's phone behind on the charger, lying on the bed.

"I'm sure there wasn't this much stuff when you moved in, Girlie," Mr Purri said. "What are we doing about the fridge?"

"Oh, we'll just leave it for the next people," Rani said. "It's a bit tatty now anyway."

Leena nods at her mum distractedly.

"See you at graduation. Oh, the boys will be, won't they?" Leena says.

"What boys?" Rani asks suspiciously.

"Just some boys from university that I did not get a chance to say goodbye to. That's all mum," Leena replies quickly.

The family leave and Janie is left alone in the flat. She continues to pack up her property. As she is packing she takes a pile of books off the table and there is the note.

"Oh shit," Janie says to herself. "Never mind I'll post it to her."

Janie quickly writes Leena's home address on the envelope and puts it aside to post later. She then continues to pack up her things.

Part Four

Chapter Thirty-Three

"Leena," Rani shouts, "can you come downstairs please, we want to talk to you for a minute."

Reluctantly Leena goes down to the living room but she looks with suspicion at her mother and then turns her gaze to her father. He is standing in front of the fireplace with a determined look on his face.

"Take a seat, Leena," Lion says.

Leena can't believe it is only a few weeks since she left university, but it seemed like a lifetime. It is now early August and she is feeling smothered by the lack of freedom, compared to living with Janie in Brighton. Leena goes over to the sofa and sits down, looking apprehensive.

"We have found a husband for Leena; the wedding is going to be in September."

"But Dad, I told you, I don't want to get married." Leena stands up and faces her father, her hands going to her hips as she thrusts her chin forward. "How could you?

"There'll be no argument this time, Leena. It's all arranged," Lion replies.

"Did you know about this?" Leena demands.

"Yes, Leena, but it will be all right, you will like this boy." Rani looks imploringly at her daughter. "I know you will ..."

"I won't," Leena answers. "I don't want to get married. I want a career."

"You can still have a career, Leena," Lion says. "At least meet the boy, he's coming over to see us tonight."

"I don't want to meet him." Leena cannot believe that this is happening to her again. "I thought that you understood. I don't want to get married yet."

Tears spring to Leena's eyes as she storms off upstairs and slams her bedroom door. Lion and Rani stand and stare at each other.

"We should tell her who it is," Rani says. "She's so upset."

"She'll find out tonight," Lion replies with a shrug. "Bad-tempered girl."

"I'll go up and talk to her," Rani says.

"No, Rani."

"I must, she's still my little girl."

Rani leaves the room and goes up the stairs to Leena but Lion turns away and smiles to himself.

"She'll be happy when she sees who it is. I know she will."

Chapter Thirty-Four

Lion, Rani and Sevi are sitting on the sofa looking grim. Rani is fussing over a plate of samosas and onion bargees that are on the side table. Lion gets up and goes over to the stairs.

"Leena, come down now please," he shouts up, but there is no answer from Leena and she doesn't come down. The doorbell rings and Rani moves towards the door but Lion stops her and goes out to answer it himself.

"You found your way, all right?" Lion asks.

"Yes Sir, your directions were very good," Alum replies.

"Rani, Sevi, this is Alum. Alum, may I present my wife, Rani, and my son, Sevi."

"Hello, Mrs Purri, Sevi. I am pleased to meet you. Where's Leena?"

"Leena is in her room and won't come down. Stubborn girl," Lion says shrugging his shoulders.

"Oh. Yes, she is stubborn. But I do love her," Alum says with a smile and then shakes Lion's hand.

Alum sits down on the sofa and looks around; he grins at Mrs Purri. "Leena often talked about you. And we always looked forward to, Mrs Purri's cooking; those cool bags were a godsend."

Rani smiled with pleasure.

"I'm very glad someone enjoyed them," Rani says.

"We most certainly did, Mrs Purri."

"Do you love my daughter, Alum?" Rani asks.

"Yes, I believe I do, very much," Alum replies.

"I knew that when I received your note," Lion says. "I know that it was not intended for me. But because it was addressed to L Purri, I opened it and then I contacted your family. I like you, boy, and I remember you from when you helped me with my car. Do you remember?"

"Yes, I do, Sir. But I did not know it was you until just now," Alum shrugs and runs his hands through his hair. "How strange, so you are Leena's father?"

"You two have met?" Sevi asks, "When? Where? So that was the reason for all the secrecy."

"Yes, we met in Brighton when your dad's car was having problems. The exhaust, if I remember rightly?

"Yes, we've met, Sevi. When I opened Alum's letter I remembered him and decided to meet his parents and we arranged for Leena and Alum to get together."

"And you know Leena from university?

"Yes. We were friends," Alum says and then smiles to himself.

"And you still want to marry her? You're very brave," Sevi says, with a smile.

Sevi and Alum laugh together but Rani looks on with a serious expression on her face and she glances toward the stairs.

"I'll go up and get Leena," Rani says as she moves towards the stairs.

Alum stands up and turns towards Rani.

"May I go?" he asks then he turns back to Lion. "Would that be all right with you, Sir? May I go up to Leena?

Lion and Rani exchange a glance and then Lion nods to Alum.

"It's the first on the right at the top of the stairs," he says.

Alum crosses the room and goes up the stairs to Leena's room. Rani looks at her husband and they smile at each other. Sevi watches them questioningly.

"She knows him. Why didn't you tell me?" he asks.

"I couldn't tell you because I knew that you would have told Leena," Lion replies, "Because you would have told her, that's why. Even if we had asked you not to, you would have given the game away. You wouldn't have been able to resist."

"No, I wouldn't …" Sevi splutters. "Well, maybe I would." he pauses. "I wish I could be a fly on the wall up there." He looks upwards as if he could see through the ceiling. "Wow."

The Purri family fall silent and wait for the explosion or the joy or the tears …. How would Leena respond?

Chapter Thirty-Five

A furious Leena is standing looking out the window in her usual hands on hips stance.

"How could they do this to me?" she mutters to herself.

Outside the window in the next door garden Mrs Price is hanging out her washing. She is humming a little tune, unaware that she was being watched.

"It's okay for you," Leena says, thinking about Dawn and Benji. "Well, maybe not so …"

Then suddenly there is a knock at the door.

"Go away; I don't want to see anybody," she growls.

There is another knock, harder this time.

"I said, 'go away'."

"Can I come in?"

Leena spins around and walks over to the door; with a violent lurch she opens it, and is ready to yell at whosoever is standing there. Her face froze as a look of complete shock replaces the anger.

"What? What are you doing here?"

"It's nice to see you to."

"But... It's just that I did not expect to see you. Mum and Dad have arranged a marriage for me and they were trying to get me to go downstairs, for when … he was coming to meet me…" Suddenly a look of comprehension came to Leena's face. "It's you, is it?" She says and bursts into tears. "No, it can't be you."

"Come on now, Greenie. It's not so bad, you know. I do love you."

"I thought…" she sobs, "I thought …"

"I tried to see you before end of term but you had left to go to the station and I missed you. I left a note. I tried to phone," he pauses. "I've been in America."

"Janie told me but, but … I never got the note," Leena stutters. "I thought you … I thought you didn't care."

"I do care, Greenie. I love you. The note went to your dad and he phoned and then he came to meet my folks. I met your dad once in Brighton. I helped him with his car," Alum says. Then Alum drops to his knees and takes Leena's hand in his. "I love you, Leena, will you marry me?"

"Oh Alum, but... Why did you not say anything before?"

"I know this is a bit back-to-front. I wanted to see you, to tell you but your parents insisted it was to be kept secret ... but Leena, my darling girl, this will be the last... the last ever secret between us. Will you marry me?" The look on Alum's face was so worried and so appealing. "I wanted you before but ... I wanted to get to know you better but you always said that you were not interested in men..." he hesitates, "or getting married."

"Alum, I..."

"I tried to phone you so many times but there was never any answer," Alum says getting to his feet, "but then I went to the USA, and things happened so fast."

"I lost my phone. I think I left it in Brighton."

"Do you love me, Leena?"

"Yes, you fool, of course I love you," she answers, "I love you. I love you, I love you."

"And will you marry me?"

Leena flings herself into Alum's arms and they kiss. Then he pushes her away from him and holds her at arm's length, looking intently into her eyes.

"Is that a yes, then?" he asks.

"Yes, yes, yes. I will marry you."

He pulls her close once more and they kiss again, then Leena stands back from Alum and looks seriously up into his face.

"I'll want to work, and where will we live? I won't live with your family and..."

"That's more like the Leena I know. Demanding the facts..." she stops his words with a kiss.

"Darling Leena, I think we will always argue but promise me something."

"What?" Leena asks.

"We won't ever let it part us. We'll learn to agree to disagree. And we will never go to bed cross with each other!"

"Yes, my love." Leena looks up at him demurely, but a cheeky grin comes to her face as she draws him near. "I'll never want us to argue, my darling," But over Alum's shoulder she has a big smile on her face.

Later that evening Leena sat down on her bed and wrote in her diary.

Leena's diary (10th August)

Well, I am amazed. Alum has just left and we are going to be married. I can't believe it. Apparently he - Alum that is – met my dad last year down on Brighton beachfront. Dad was having trouble with the car or something and Alum helped him.

We are going to be married. I love him. I think I've always loved him. He was so cute; he got down on his knees and asked me to marry him. Not like the arrogant Alum I knew in university. I always liked him but I thought he just ... well I don't know what I thought ... he just always seemed to disagree with anything I said. He teased me but he was never unkind.

I have been so unhappy since I finished university, I thought he didn't care. Mum and Dad have been so protective and unchallenging. But I've been feeling so suffocated. Even when I mentioned going on that work experience study in Africa they said. "There's plenty of time. Wait until the autumn; we have only just got you home." Now I know why.

Also granny dying at the end of July has made for a subdued atmosphere in the house. Apparently she has left a bit of a financial tangle to sort out. Dad had to go off to St Albans for few days to help Aunty Kalpane and her husband sort out Gran's house which was being rented to a housing association, but they still managed to arrange this marriage and keep it from me.

They kept it very quiet. I wonder if Sevi knew - I doubt it, he wouldn't have been able to resist telling me.

Bloody hell; Alum loves me and we are going to get married!
I must phone Janie.

Chapter Thirty-Six

Three months later the local community hall is buzzing. Linda and Fay arrive and weave their way in through the crowd of people. They see Pretti and Rajput with their children; now aged two and a half and seven months.

"Pretti, you look wonderful. How are you?" Linda exclaims.

"I'm very well. You know Rajput and this is little Rafi and Jamilla my beautiful little princess," Pretti says.

They look extremely happy and Pretti is dressed in a beautiful pale blue sari and looking very conservative.

At that moment Benji also arrives with his girlfriend, Dawn, followed by Mr and Mrs Price and Jim. Jim immediately runs over to Sevi.

"Oh, aren't they beautiful, Pretti," Fay says, bending down to Pretti's children.

The little girl, now two and a half, is looking up at them in awe with huge brown eyes and the baby boy is asleep in the pushchair.

"We think so, don't we, Pretti?" Rajput answers, looking lovingly at his wife.

Linda also bends down to look at the children. Benji wanders over with Dawn and they stand listening. Linda greets Dawn and Benji and then sits down and watches as throngs of people are arriving.

"Hello, little ones, don't you look cute," Dawn says.

Pretti and Rajput look at each other and smile happily, seeming full of pride at their beautiful children.

"Oh, look at their outfits, just adorable," Fay enthuses.

"Rajput's mother bought them in India," Pretti replies smugly.

"That's nice," Fay says. "Are you getting on okay?"

"Yes. We are getting on well now," Pretti says glancing up at Rajput with a shy smile.

"Oh, that's good," Fay says, starting to look around at the festivities. "The hall looks amazing, don't you think?"

"Yes, just lovely," Pretti says demurely. "They deserve it. I hope they will be very happy."

"Right," Fay murmurs as she turns back to Dawn with a grin, "they do."

In a different area of the hall Jim confronts Sevi.

"What do you look like, *bro*?" Jim says, "A little prince?"

"I know, but Mum insisted," Sevi replies.

"No, it's cool *in' it*. Do you think I can get Dawn and Benji to have a traditional Indian wedding; then I can borrow your costume," Jim replies cheekily.

"Your mum might have something to say about that. Is she okay? I mean, has she accepted their relationship?"

"Well. I think she's gonna to have to. Dawn is adamant. I mean Benji is a great guy." Jim grins. "And my dad's on their side. And since he has the new job, Dad that is, as a lecturer in a local college, he's standing up to Mum a bit more."

"That's great, I like Benji, he's cool," Sevi says waving his arm towards the central platform, "and he's not very traditional, is he? I mean he wouldn't want all this palaver, would he?"

'I don't think so. It might be fun though, if just to see my mum in a sari."

They burst out laughing and a few heads turned towards them.

"I'll see if my mum will lend her one." Sevi laughs and then looks around towards his father. "I'd better go. I have to be there when the couple arrive. See you later, Jim."

"I'm going to talk to that pretty girl."

Jim points over to where a small group of youngsters are standing. And one girl in particular is looking their way.

"Good luck with that," Sevi murmurs as he dashes off toward the entrance.

The local community hall has been transformed, there are decorations hanging from the walls, huge vases of flowers in every corner and there is the *Madap*, or canopy, on a platform in the centre of the hall decorated with fresh flowers and golden garlands made from paper and foil.

"It's great to see you, we will get together and have a good chat later," Linda says as she stands up again and embraces Pretti.

"We'll see you after the ceremony," Rajput says as he takes control of the pushchair and heads off with Pretti towards some other guests.

Pretti turns and looks at Dawn.

"We must get together and talk about your wedding," she says. "Are you going to do something like this?"

"I don't think so, Pretti," Dawn answers with a quick look at Benji who is talking to Fay. "We must do that, get together that is. I doubt we'll do the huge Indian wedding thing; just a simple ceremony down at the Town Hall."

"That's a shame," Pretti says wistfully. "I do regret not having the big traditional wedding, but we are happy."

"Do you?"

"Well, off course I do, what girl wouldn't want a lovely big wedding with all her friends there?" Pretti replies.

"I suppose so," Dawn says. "But I honestly don't really care where we get married as long as we can get married."

"Are your parents being difficult?"

"Yes, well no. Dad's fine with it, but Mum is a bit of a … Well, you know how it is."

"Yes, I do. We had our problems at first," Pretti smiled. "But if you really love each other you can get past the obstacles."

"I'm sure that's true," Dawn replies.

"Come my love, I want you to meet my friend, Jackie," Rajput interrupts, appearing behind Pretti and taking her arm.

"See you later," Pretti calls as she is led away towards a group of young men near the door.

"Righty oh," Dawn replies turning towards Benji and Fay.

After they had moved a safe distance away Benji nudges Dawn.

"Well, you never know how things are going to work out," Benji says quietly to Dawn. "My parents may insist on a proper Indian style wedding."

"Do you think so?" Dawn replies looking scared. "What do you think, Fay?"

Fay was standing watching Pretti and Rajput as they walked off towards the back of the hall.

"Yes, who would have guessed? Pretti and Rajput together and Pretti looking just like the model Indian wife? I would never have thought…" Fay says.

"Of course, I knew they were seeing each other ages ago," Benji interrupts Fay with a grin then turns and winks at Dawn.

"Well, she sure kept it quiet from us. I was flabbergasted when they ran off together," Linda says.

"It all worked out for the best." Fay smiles looking around at the crowds of people who are now arriving. "You look great, Dawn. I love that outfit."

"It's stunning - your own design?" Linda asks.

"Yes. I am working on my own range of clothes and Benji's dad is getting them made up in India," Dawn replies.

"I love it, and well done you! And thanks for making this up for me." Linda swirls the beautiful silk skirt that Dawn had made for her.

"No problem, it looks great," Dawn replies.

"I want to see what's going on over there," Fay says then she waves her arm in the direction of the *Madap*, where Roopa is standing adjusting some bowls. "See you later, Benji."

"Okay then, see you both later. Come on, Dawn, let's talk to Leena's friends from university," Benji says taking her hand and heading off towards Janie and Pieter. "They are looking a bit lost."

"Okay darling?" Dawn is looking around and taking it all in, probably still feeling a bit scared that Benji is serious about them having their own Indian wedding. "Would you want all this?" she asks tentatively.

"No, not really darling, but I know that my mum would," he replies.

"What?" Dawn asks. "Really?"

Benji laughs and puts his arm around Dawn's shoulders. "Don't you worry, the cost alone will put them off, all this costs a bloody fortune."

"I hope so," Dawn says quietly to herself. "I really hope so."

Both Linda and Fay have wandered over to the *Madap* and are gazing at it when Roopa comes up to them.

"Hello. Are you Leena's friends from school?" Roopa asks.

"Yes," Linda answers, "we are."

"I'm her Aunt Roopa."

"Pleased to meet you, I'm sure. I'm Fay and this is Linda," Fay says. "And that's Benji and his girlfriend. I mean, fiancée Dawn. Dawn was Leena's next door neighbour. Roopa glances at Benji and Dawn and frowns.

"I know them," she said, but then she smiles and turns her attention to the centre of the room as they all turn to gaze up at the *Madap*. "The four pillars represent the four cornerstones of love and happiness in a marriage. The right choice of partner," again she glances back at Dawn and Benji, "and a positive attitude towards each other and the world in general, an agreement to approach parenting as equal partners, and enduring love for each other," Roopa explains to the girls.

"How beautiful," Fay says.

"It is," Roopa replies and then indicates a platform with an intricate candle and flame. "Yes it is, and this is the *Agni*, which personifies the power and light of the Gods. This acts as a divine witness to the union and brings happiness throughout the married life," Roopa explains.

"Where are Leena and Alum?" asks Linda.

"They have not arrived yet but they will be here soon. Which reminds me, I must go to make sure everything is ready. See you later."

"Yes. Thank you, Roopa," Fay says. "That'd be great."

More guests are arriving every moment and Janie and Pieter call to Madge who has just walked in the door and is looking around apprehensively hoping to see someone she knows. She spots Pieter and goes over to him just as Dawn and Benji introduce themselves.

"Hello. I'm Benji and this is my wife-to-be, Dawn," Benji says turning towards Madge, causing Dawn to blush as she greets Leena's university friends.

"Pleased to meet you," Janie replies.

"Dawn is Leena's next door neighbour," Benji continues taking Dawn's hand and giving it a squeeze.

"I'm pleased to meet you," Madge says. "This is Janie and Pieter and I am Madge. I was Alum's landlady for three years."

"Really, then you can tell us all his nasty secrets?" Benji asks.

"Well, he was a model tenant, and worked very hard, from what I saw."

"That's no fun, we want some dirt," Benji winked at Pieter.

"Well you won't get it from me," she retorts. "He was a joy and I miss him terribly."

"What, no mischief or naughty goings on?" Benji quipped.

At that moment Eggs enters the hall and joins his friends.

"Hello all," he says.

"Hi Eggs," Janie says, "You found the place okay then?"

"What's this I overheard about mischief?" he asks.

"We were all working too hard to get up to any mischief," Pieter says.

"Is that true?" Benji asks, turning to Janie.

"Fraid so," Janie says. "It was so very annoying."

She looks up at Pieter, who is watching her closely.

"It took me a while to realize that there was mischief to be had. I am a bit slow on the uptake sometimes."

Janie laughs and the others realise that they are missing some private joke.

"Well, are you making up for it now?" Dawn asks.

"Oh yes," Pieter says. "We sure are."

"That's okay then." Dawn smiles at Janie. "Leena's roommate; she told me all about you."

"Nothing good, I hope," Janie says cheekily then wistfully adds. "I do miss the Indian food. Leena's mum is a very good cook."

At that moment Mr and Mrs Purri enter the hall followed by Mr and Mrs Contem.

"The groom is coming," Lion yells, putting his arm around Rani to lead her back to the entrance hall. "Our beautiful girl is getting married. Where's Sevi?"

"I'm right here Dad, don't panic," Sevi says from behind him.

"Just don't wander off, my boy," Lion pronounces proudly. "Here he comes."

"Bloody hell," Sevi exclaims, "he's riding a horse!"

Chapter Thirty-Seven

Suddenly there is a rush of people to the hall's entrance and Alum's university friends are astonished to see that Alum is indeed riding a horse, a large white horse. He is surrounded by friends and relatives. He dismounts and comes to the doorway of the hall. Dressed in a dark gold tunic and white trousers, he looks extremely handsome. As he enters the hall doors he is greeted by Mr and Mrs Purri and is led in by them to face his friends and Leena's family including her Aunty Lakshmi from India, with three of her daughters and Aunty Kalpane and her husband from St Albans. Alum looks overwhelmed as many of them break into a spontaneous applause.

"Welcome Alum." Lion embraces Alum and leads him in to the hallway.
"Thank you," Alum replies politely and smiles at Lion. Then he sees Janie, Pieter, Eggs and Madge in the hall. "Would you excuse me one moment please, Sir?"
"Of course," Lion replies.
"Call me when it's time."
Alum strides over to welcome his friends, shaking Eggs' and Pieter's hands and kissing Janie and Madge on the cheek.
"My friends," he says, "I'm so glad you could make it."
"We would not have missed this for the world," Pieter answers grasping Alum's arm.
"You look fantastic, Alum, but the horse?" Eggs says, his eyes open wide in wonder. "We didn't expect that…"
"Tradition mate, we couldn't find an elephant," he shrugs. "The family arranged it."
"You look very fetching," Janie says.
"Good to see you, man. Finally got it together then?" Pieter exclaims.
Alum grins at Pieter but turns aside as he notices Dawn and Benji.
"I'm Dawn, Leena's next door neighbour and this is my fiancé, Benji."

"Pleased to meet you, Leena has spoken of you often," Alum says shaking Benji's hand and giving Dawn a quick peck on the cheek before turning back to Pieter. "Yes, thanks to you, old mate, and a few false starts, but we're getting there," Alum winks at Janie. "And you two. What's happening with you?"

At that moment Alum's father comes up behind him and taps him on the shoulder.
"Alum, your bride is coming, you must get into position."
"See you all later," Alum says. "I want to know everything!" He then stops and turns back to Janie and Pieter. "I will want to hear all about you two and your travels. I'll talk to you later, Madge, and Eggs, thank you both so very much for coming."
"Thank you for inviting me Alum," Madge says. "Congratulations on your First and Leena too, you must both be proud."
"I am," he replies. "Leena really deserved it; she worked so hard."

Alum went off with his father toward the *Madap* and then there's a commotion near the entrance as the bridal party get ready to enter.
"He looks happy," Janie observes.
"And so he should, Leena is a fantastic girl," Pieter says.
"No regrets?" Janie asks.
"No regrets, my darling. I love you, don't be a silly goose." Pieter puts his arm around Janie and they turn towards Madge and Tim. "Let go watch this wedding. There were times I never believed that it was actually going to happen."
"Me too," Janie replies as they head off towards the hall's entrance. "Here comes Leena. Oh my god. She looks so beautiful."
"Wow," Pieter says. "Alum is a lucky man." Janie nudges Pieter in the ribs and he gives her a hug. "Just kidding, sweetheart, I'm happy with my darling Janie."
Dawn and Benji stand aside to watch as Leena enters the hall, Dawn gasps as she sees her friend enter.
"She looks amazing," Dawn exclaims.
"She sure does," Eggs gasps.
"I love that sari," Benji says. "It must have cost a fortune."

"It's fabulous; I think her Aunty Lakshmi sent it from India." Dawn sighs. "Oh Benji she looks like a princess."

"Are you having second thoughts about an Indian wedding, Babe?"

"No. I could never carry it off like Leena."

As Leena enters everybody turns to watch. She is wearing a stunning red sari with gold and silver beading around the border. There is a lot of gold jewellery and henna on her hands and she does indeed look beautiful. She walks into the hall and is led by her father to the *Madap*. With her is Sevi all dressed up in navy blue and gold in traditional costume and looking so proud and self-important. He glances over at his friend Jim and winks. Jim and his parents stand near Pretti and watch in awe at the spectacle before them. Benji and Dawn join them.

"I hope you two aren't planning anything like this," Mrs Price remarks quietly. "Although she does look incredible and he's so handsome."

"No Mum, it's far too expensive," Dawn replies, winking at her dad. "We will just run away to Gretna Green like Pretti."

"No you won't," Mr Price says quickly. "I want to take my girl down the aisle, on my arm."

"Humph," Mrs Price mutters. "If we can afford …"

"Shush," Mr Price retorts as the ceremony starts and the guests start to gather around the *Madap*.

Leena and Alum greet each other and exchange flower garlands. *Veda Mantras*, the religious rhymes of the Hindu faith, are chanted. Leena and Alum then stand on the platform and Leena offers Alum a mixture of honey and yoghurt, water is flicked symbolically three times on to the platform.

Aunt Roopa appears at Linda and Fay's side.

"The honey and yogurt represent commitment and sweetness in life, it is called *madhu parka*. And the water is for purification of the heart and body. It is called *aachamn*," she tells them quietly.

Coloured treads are then tied on to Leena and Alum's wrists. Then Leena's parents place her right hand on that of Alum giving their consent to the marriage.

"Now the sacred fire is kindled and an offering is made," Roopa murmurs.

"What does that mean?" Fay whispers back to Roopa.

"The flame is the spirit of the gods and they are making an offering to invoke the blessing of the gods.The offering is ghee and a mixture of herbs and spices. It is called *havan*," Roopa replies quietly.

Alum then takes the hand of his bride and they both make a solemn pledge before their gods that they have become one and will forever love each other. They circle the fire four times, the first three led by the bride and then the forth led by the groom. The bride and groom step on a stone after each circle and offer prayers for their marriage. Sevi places rice into the hands of his sister, Leena, then presents the rice to the flame.

"The stone makes the marriage firm as stone. And the four steps represent the four stages of life. *Dharma*, religious duty, *Artha*, Wealth, *Kama*, fulfilment of worldly desires and *Moksha*, salvation," Roopa tells the girls. Roopa is enjoying herself, showing off and sharing her knowledge and claiming her part in this wedding that she did not instigate.

"Then they take seven steps and with each step they make a vow to each other."

Leena and Alum recite the vow together as they gaze into each other's eyes.

"Our love becomes firm with this first step. We will cherish and care for each other. We will give each other strength and courage. We will share our joys and sorrows. We will care for our children. We will share in knowledge, happiness and harmony with body, mind and soul." Leena pauses and then they begin again. "With the seventh step our love and friendship will become eternal. We have spiritual union in the presence of God. These promises are made with a pure mind and we will love each other forever."

Alum puts the sindoor red powder in the hair parting and forehead of his bride and he also puts a heavy gold necklace around her neck. His fingers brush Leena's shoulder and she shivers and looks up at him her eyes glowing dark with emotion.

"I know this one. The red powder is the mark of a married woman," Fay says, tears coming to her eyes. "It's so beautiful."

"That's right and the necklace is also a symbol of the marriage and the groom's love for his new wife," Roopa says.

Roopa also cries as Leena and Alum are pronounced man and wife.

"I love to see my young people matched up. It brings me such joy, even if I didn't do the introducing in this case. I have investigated the family and they seem ..."

There is a sudden rush of relatives and guests and the last hymns are recited and then a shower of fresh flowers is tossed over the couple.

"That's to wish them luck," Roopa says, her voice muffled as she wipes away tears with a bright red silk handkerchief.

"Yes, I know it's the same with our weddings," Fay replies glancing over at Pieter and Janie. "Who's that?" she asks, "the tall blond guy."

"Who's what?" Linda asks, looking around at Janie. "Oh, that's Leena's flatmate from university and her boyfriend, Pieter, I think."

"Shame, he's gorgeous," Fay says, still gazing over at Pieter. "But the other guy is cute as well."

The reception continues and a series of trestle tables are uncovered to reveal mountains of food. More containers appear from the kitchen containing hot dishes, including nan bread, dhal, curries and rice. At the other end of the hall a bar opens and on the stage a band is setting up their equipment. Everywhere people are talking and getting to know each other.

Leena and Alum are greeting and talking to their guests. Pretti and Rajput are dancing and playing with their little girl, who seems to be having a great time. But after a while the baby starts to cry and Jamilla seems to be getting bit tired, so Pretti and Rajput start preparing to leave. Before they go Pretti and Rajput go over to Leena and Alum.

"I do wish you joy," Pretti says, "and you look so beautiful. I would have loved a big wedding like this but …"

"Thank you, Pretti, if we are as happy as you seem to be, I'll be content."

"Thank you very much, Leena. But we do have to go, the children are getting tired," Pretti says, bending to tuck a blanket around her little baby boy.

"Thank you for coming, goodbye Rajput," Leena says.

"Thank you for being so understanding, Leena … I do wish you both every happiness. You are a lucky man Alum."

"I know." Alum gazes at Leena and smiles and turns his gaze back to Pretti and Rajput. "I'm very pleased to meet you both, goodbye Pretti, goodbye Rajput."

Pretti and Rajput and their children leave the hall. As they go through the door Pretti turns and glances back at Leena and Alum. And she smiles at Leena. "You did well," she mouths silently to Leena. "Be happy."

Janie comes up besides Leena. "Is that the one?" she asks. "Is that the notorious Pretti?"

"Yes, that's Pretti. She seems very content … I think she's happy now," Leena says and she turns to Janie. "And you, are you happy?"

"Oh yes, Leena. We're very happy," Janie says with a cheerful smile. "In fact, I think I'll go grab my man for a dance before one of your friends nabs him."

Pieter is talking to Fay and Linda. Fay is looking very interested in the blond stranger.

"Good idea," Leena says to herself as she takes Alum's arm and pulls him away from Roopa who had come up to him and was asking all sort of pertinent questions about his prospects.

"Please excuse me," Alum says addressing Roopa and then turning to Leena, "Wife?"

"Yes, husband," Leena replies demurely. "Hello Roopa," she says. "I hope you are well."

"I'm very well. Be happy beautiful girl," Roopa smiles at Leena. "I approve of your handsome husband," she whispers.

"I'm glad you approve," Leena replies taking Alum's arm and looking up lovingly into his eyes.

Roopa discreetly moves away and Alum puts his arms around his new bride.

"I love you. I never dreamed that I could love you so much, but I do."

"And, I love you too, very much. I can't believe this is real," Leena smiles.

"It's real, my darling, it's real. Would you like to dance?" He then grabs her around the waist and spins her off towards the dancing area. Leena puts her head on his shoulder and they circle the floor oblivious to the hustle and bustle of the merrymaking all around them.

"I love you," she murmurs into his neck.

"Ditto," he replies. "Mrs Contem."

"I could never have believed that I could be so happy."

"Believe, little Greenie, believe."

"Alum," Leena exclaims, her head rising from his shoulder and her face perplexed. "You …"

But he stops her mouth with a kiss and she relaxes against him. He has found the perfect way to stem her words and she relaxes back against him snuggling into his neck in contentment.

When Leena looks over Alum's shoulder she sees that Janie and Pieter and Dawn and Benji are dancing together and her friend Linda is dancing with Eggs and Fay is chatting to Aunty Roopa. Madge is talking to another guest and some of the children are running about enjoying the festivities. Leena can't see Sevi but then she spots him with Jim in the corner talking to a couple of girls. Aunty Lakshmi is dancing with one of her daughters and Aunty Kalpane.

Smiling to herself she pulls Alum close; the party is really getting going. The band is now playing some modern pop music and the younger members at the get-together are having a great time. Lion drags a protesting Rani on to the dance floor and is attempting to dance, much to Rani's embarrassment. After a short time Leena, safe and content in her husband's arms, is oblivious of the celebration going on around her.

Leena's diary (September 20th)

Well. Here I am on my honeymoon in Crete; that was a big surprise. I did not even know we were going on a honeymoon. Dad paid for it out of the money from his mother's estate and gave us the tickets at the wedding. Crete is so beautiful; we are going on a trip to the other side of the island tomorrow to visit some caves.

Alum is still asleep. He looks so gorgeous in the morning, even with his hair all ruffled and untidy. Gosh, I love him so much. I still can't quite believe it, we are married.

We had a wonderful ceremony at the local community hall and all my friends came, Janie, Pieter, Eggs and Alum's landlady Madge from university. Pretti and Rajput came with their two children; they are so cute. Linda and Fay, Dawn with Benji and the Prices. Dawn and Benji are getting married next month in the local registry office. Luckily I – we will be back by then, I would not want to miss that.

It will be a quiet affair, not like my wedding. Alum arrived on a horse, can you believe it and Sevi and the family were all dressed up, it looked fabulous. Even Aunty Lakshmi came from India with three of her daughters. Thank goodness the weather was warm or they would have frozen in their saris. Aunty Kalpane was there but she was a bit withdrawn, it was good to see her and she cheered up when she was with the family.

And I had great news the day before we came away, I received a response from Water Aid and I have a second interview the week after we get home. They do such good work for women in Africa who have to walk miles to get fresh water. It would be a great job and I would get to travel. Alum has a good job and we can soon afford to buy a place of our own. It's going to be great. I am very happy. Alum is the best.

Oops, Alum is waking up, I had better get ready for breakfast. That is, if he doesn't want another lie in. One of the best things about being married is waking up in the morning next to my gorgeous husband and not getting up. Alum is so cuddly and tender in the bed department, so sexy! Who would have thought!

Yes, it's back to bed; must go.

Leena and Alum go on to be very happy, they spend the rest of their lives together, they will always argue, but agree never to take their quarrel to bed.

"Each day a fresh start," Alum would say.

THE END

Personal Profile: Linda Louisa Dell

Linda left school at 15 with no qualifications, mildly dyslexic. She has lived most of her life in North West London. She was a model in her teens and twenties doing photographic and promotion work.

Linda went to University in 1992 to study Spanish, Science and Technology at Middlesex University for four years and she has travelled extensively in Central and South America including a ten month stay in Costa Rica studying at the University of Costa Rica, after which she spent a further six months travelling through Central and South America and in Trinidad and Tobago where she wrote her Spanish thesis on the History of Carnival in Trinidad.

For the last 18 years she has practised as a holistic therapist with her own practice in Hendon and working two days per week for the John Lewis Partnership doing massage and reflexology therapy for the staff. She did a writing course with the Writers Bureau and has also completed four short Open University courses which she found very useful.

Linda writes articles and short stories and has had several printed in magazines such as: The Lady, Prediction, Yours, Fate and Fortune, Here's Heath and Holistic Health and Healing magazines.

Her first book; *Can't Sleep Won't Sleep* (Reasons and remedies for insomnia) took three years to research and write and was published in 2005. Her second book; *Dreamtime* (A History, Mythology, Physiology and Guide to the Interpretation of Dreams) published in 2008. Her third book; *Aphrodisiacs, Aphrodite's Secrets,* (Sexuality, Sexual dysfunction, history and anecdotal use of aphrodisiacs) published in 2009 and *The A-Z of Aphrodisiacs* May 2015 from the New York publisher, Skyhorse.

She has also written and self-published three novels: *Yes and Pigs Might Fly*, finalist in the Wishing Shelf best fiction awards 2012 set in England and Greece; *African Nights,* an adventure and love story set in London and in South Africa, and *Earthscape; a long way from home*, a sci-fi adventure and romance.

Linda has also self-published a joke book, *Jokes* a collection of short stories, T*he Story Tree*; a collection of poetry, *My Poetry*; as well as several e-books on sleep problems and dreams.

Please see her web page for more information:
www.lindalouisadell.com